Frank M. Lupton

The Mystic Oracle

The complete fortune-teller and dream book

Frank M. Lupton

The Mystic Oracle
The complete fortune-teller and dream book

ISBN/EAN: 9783337370398

Printed in Europe, USA, Canada, Australia, Japan

Cover: Foto ©Andreas Hilbeck / pixelio.de

More available books at **www.hansebooks.com**

21.
PRICE, TEN CENTS.

Published Semi monthly. By Subscription, $2.40 Per Annum. November 1, 1893.
Entered at the New York Post Office as Second-Class Matter. Copyright, 1893, by F. M. Lupton.

THE PEOPLE'S HAND BOOK SERIES

The Mystic Oracle;

OR, THE

Complete Fortune-Teller and Dream Book.

✳

F. M. LUPTON.
PUBLISHER.
106 AND 108 READE ST.,
NEW YORK.

The Mystic Oracle;

OR, THE

COMPLETE FORTUNE-TELLER AND DREAM-BOOK.

BOOK THE FIRST.

ZODIÆOLOGY;

Or, the Science of foretelling Events by a consideration of the Signs of the Zodiac, the Sun and Moon, and the Planetary System.—With Lists of Lucky and Unlucky Days and Presages drawn therefrom.

THAT man at the moment of his birth receives the lurking principle of death—

" The young disease, that must subdue at length,
Grows with his growth, and strengthens with his strength,"

is as acknowledged an axiom as that nothing in this world is immutable—and it is as fully acknowledged by daily observation and experience, that the fate of every person in existence is written in the heavens, at the time of each of their births—and that the sun, moon, and stars, have a visible effect upon the future occurrences of our lives, by shedding their genial and malign influence upon us at the moment of our first entrance into it. In order, therefore, that any person may learn from a consideration of the situation of the sign of the heavens at the time of their birth, what is contained for them in the book of fate, it will be necessary for them to cast their nativity—the manner of doing this is as follows:—

Having ascertained the exact time of your birth, and the hour in which you entered this transitory life, procure a Moore's Almanac of the year, which will direct you to the sign that then reigned, the name of the planet, and the state of the moon; particularly observe whether the sun was just entering the sign, whether it was near the end, or what was its particular 'rogress: if at the beginning, your fate will be strongly tinctured with its properties, moderate .t the meridian, and slightly if the sun is nearly going out of the sign.

Write down the day of the week, see whether it is a lucky day or not, the state of the moon, the nature of the planets, and the influence described next, and you will, by making your observations, ascertain your future destiny with very little trouble.

Thus from a judicious and accurate observation of the position of the planets at the moment when we first respire the breath of life, may easily be gathered what kind of existence our destiny has decreed for us—what propensities will distinguish our career—what pursuits will mark our way, and what success we may reasonably expect to attend our exertions. Thus, an education suited to our particular genius and talents may be given us, and we may thereby be enabled to turn many of those distinguishing peculiarities, which more or less stamp all the beings of the human species, to our advantage and happiness, that for want of this necessary information might become the sources of our wretchedness and misery.

We are enabled to afford our readers some useful and entertaining discoveries on the effect of the planets over the race of man; and as the Sun is the most powerful and conspicuous, we shall proceed to mark his way through the different signs of the zodiac, and to show the effect of his revolutions, beginning, for the sake of enabling our readers more readily to find what they may want, with the month of January although the ancients began their year be March. ter-

JANUARY.

Aquarius, or the Water-bearer.

About the twentieth of the month the sun enters this sign: a man born at this period will be of an unruly, restless, fickle, and boisterous disposition; will be given to odd whims and strange fancies; will undertake any thing, however difficult, to accomplish any object he may have in view; not contented long in one place; soon affronted—slow to forgive; suspicious and always imagining danger, and, instead of endeavoring to subdue trouble, meeting it half way. In life he will be moderately successful, and enjoy a portion of happiness. In love he will display an amorous disposition, and be passionately attached to his mistress, until she yields to his wishes, or marries him; he will then grow indifferent, and rove until some other object fixes his attention.

A woman born at this time will be of a studious, industrious, and sedentary disposition—will be much attached to the employment she is brought up to; in love she will be constant and moderate—she will make a kind and tender mother, and an affectionate wife.

FEBRUARY.

Pisces, or the Fishes.

About the twentieth of the month the sun enters this sign: a man born at this time will be designing, intriguing, selfish, unfaithful to his engagements; he will be mean, and subservient to those whom he thinks he can make useful to his schemes; but his end once obtained, he will take every opportunity to injure and betray them: in poverty he will be a sycophant, in prosperity a tyrant—haughty to equals and inferiors. In life he will generally be unsuccessful, although for a time he will often appear to have succeeded: in love he will be careless, indifferent, and unsteady—he will make a severe father, and an unkind husband.

A woman born at the same period will be of obliging manners, delicate in her ideas, open, and sincere in her friendships, an enemy to deceit—in love she will be faithful, and moderately inclined to the joys of Venus: she will be affectionate to her family; make a good and tender mother and be a prosperous and excellent wife.

MARCH.

Aries, or the Ram.

bout the twentieth of the month the sun rs this sign; a man born at this period will ᵤᵤ of a bashful, meek, and irresolute disposition, hard to provoke to a quarrel, but difficult to be appeased when roused: in life he will be for the most part happy and contented—in love he will be faithful and constant, moderately addicted to its pleasures—he will be a kind, affectionate father, a good husband, a sincere friend, and of an industrious turn.

A woman born at the same time will be modest, chaste, good-tempered, cleanly in her habits, industrious, and charitable—in love she will be faithful, and in life she will be rather happy than· otherwise, but be little concerned about worldly affairs—she will make an amiable mother, be decently fond of her husband, and moderately given to the joys of Hymen.

APRIL.

Taurus, or the Bull.

About the twentieth of the month the sun enters this sign: a man born at this time will be of a strong and robust constitution, faithful to his engagements, industrious, sober, and honest, but prone to anger—in life he will be ardent in his pursuits, but will meet with many vexations and disappointments—in love he will be extremely amorous, much given to women, of a jealous disposition, liable to infidelity to the marriage bed, but on the whole a good husband, and a kind father—he will be extremely desirous of roving in the world, and establishing a reputation.

A woman born at this period will be of a courageous and resolute disposition, of an industrious turn, impatient of control, desirous of praise, and not easily daunted, fond of domestic life, much attached to those pleasures that are consistent with virtue, fond of her husband, indulgent to her children, and a sincere friend, and liberal benefactress—she will be happy in the connubial state, and pass her time with much satisfaction.

MAY.

Gemini, or the Twins.

About the twentieth of the month the sun en ters this sign: a man born at this period will be of an undaunted courage, of a sweet and cheerful temper, of a lively imagination, stern in his resentments, though not easily provoked—he will be very ambitious of distinguishing himself for his learning and his knowledge of his profession or trade—in life he will be inclined to traveling, especially in foreign countries—he will meet with many crosses, and much persecution, but will bear them all with manly fortitude, and great patience—he will be immoderately attached to women, placing all his happiness in their arms—he will make a good father, but an unfaithful husband.

A woman born at this period will be of a peevish and fretful temper—she will be vindictive and revengeful, not very industrious, but inclined to neatness in dress and in her house —in love she will be credulous and jealous, much inclined to the pleasures of the marriage bed—in life she will meet with many disagreeable interruptions to her peace of mind, but be of a generous disposition, kind to her children, affectionate to her husband, and liberal to her dependents.

JUNE.

Cancer, or the Crab.

About the twentieth of the month the sun en· ters this sign: a man born at this period will be of an industrious and sober disposition, diffident of his own abilities, not easily excited to mirth, firm and inflexible in his determinations—in life, he will be faithful to his engagements, successful in his pursuits, and kind to his fellow-creatures—in love he will be sincere, moderately inclined to the joys of Hymen, faithful to the nuptial bed, a tender father, and a kind husband.

A woman born at this time will be of a captious temper inclined to industry, and fond of merriment and good cheer—in life she will be persevering in her undertakings, tenacious of her own opinion, but without provoking obstinacy—she will be much inclined to the pleasures of love in a lawful manner, will make a good wife, and an affectionate mother, and enjoy a reasonable share of happiness and tranquillity.

JULY.

Leo, or the Lion.

About the twentieth of the month the sun enters this sign: a man born at this period will be of an unruly, turbulent, rapacious, and quarrelsome disposition, always inclined to dispute with his neighbors, and enter into lawsuits—in life he will be for ever scheming, without accomplishing his ends; he will be troublesome to others and to himself, and for the most part be unhappy—in love he will be indifferent, making it a secondary consideration—he will be unfaithful whenever his interests so dictate—he will make a morose husband, and a negligent father.

A woman born at this time will be of an abusive and quarrelsome disposition, indolent and peevish in her temper, fond of calumniating her neighbors—she will be little inclined to the pleasures of love, be a very indifferent mother, and a sluttish wife—in life she will be perpetually in scrapes, and be for the most part unhappy herself by endeavoring to make others so.

AUGUST.

Virgo, or the Virgin.

About the twentieth of the month the sun enters this sign: a man born at this period will be of a rather a timid disposition, though not cowardly—he will be honest and sincere in his dealings, much reserved in conversation, cautious in his undertakings, good-tempered and mild, gentle in his behavior and sober in his conduct—in life, he will be tolerably happy, and moderately successful—in love he will be much inclined to lawless pleasures, yet affectionate to his wife—he will make a good father, and a tender husband.

A woman born at this time will be of a very honest, sincere, and candid disposition, much inclined to cleanliness in her person, of warm desires, modest speech, fond of connubial joys, and faithful to her husband—she will make a good mother, and an industrious wife.

SEPTEMBER.

Libra, or the Balance.

About the twentieth of the month the sun enters this sign: a man born at this period will be of an honest, sober, and upright disposition, faithful and just in his dealings, a great lover of truth, and an enemy to quarrels and disturbances—in life he will be highly respected, whatever may be his situation, rich or poor—if he arrives at honors and places of consequence, he will still retain a veneration for his old friends, protect them to the utmost of his power, and conduct himself with temper and moderation—in love he will be no enemy to the pleasures of wedlock, but make an affectionate husband and a kind father.

A woman born at this time will be of a prudent, modest, and virtuous disposition, dignified in her manners, affable and agreeable in her conversation, generous in her temper, in life she will be very happy—in the business of love she will only consider it as a duty in obedience to her husband, and will make an obedient and complying wife, and a careful and attentive mother.

OCTOBER.

Scorpio, or the Scorpion.

About the twentieth of the month the sun enters this sign: a man born at this period will be of an amiable and solid disposition, of a lively imagination, prudent in his conduct, and agreeable in his manners. In life he will be subject to many cruel and severe hardships, he will have many enemies, be suspected of plots and conspiracies against the state; he will be persecuted and calumniated, but by the interposition of friends he will be raised by his merits, in the end triumph over his enemies, and be extricated from his difficulties. In love he will be faithful and sincere, much addicted to the delights of the connubial state, but obliged to make his passions yield to his other concerns in life; he will be a fond father and an affectionate husband.

A woman born at this time will be of a rash, imperious, intriguing, and designing disposition, of an unsteady and disagreeable temper, and inclined to liquor. In life her schemes will generally miscarry through her own folly and want of conduct. In love she will yield to its pleasures only with a view to serve her purpose, and she will be fickle and unfaithful—make a bad wife, savage mother, and be the cause of her family's unhappiness.

NOVEMBER.

Sagittarius, or the Archer.

About the twentieth of the month the sun enters this sign; a man born at this period will be of a cold, phlegmatic disposition, of little sensibility, furious when in a passion, implacable in his resentments, punctual in his dealings. In life he will be generally successful, easily led by others, and frequently deceived. In love he will be moderate in his passions, caressing his wife merely for the sake of getting children, to whom he will make an excellent father, but will be a morose and tyrannical husband.

A woman born at this time will be of a masculine disposition, much addicted to calumniate others, and spreading scandalous reports of those she does not like; in her behavior she will be imperious and disagreeable, a great scold, and inclined to strong liquors and quarrelling. In life she will make many enemies by her want of conduct and little regard to what she says, be rather unhappy and unsuccessful in her pursuits. In love she will be constant, but expect to govern her husband—she will expect him to do strict justice to the marriage bed, to the pleasures of which she will be immoderately attached; she will love her children but be negligent of them—she will be fond of her husband, whilst he gives her her own way, and strictly performs the marriage rites; but if they are neglected, she will lead him a wearisome life, and prove unfaithful.

DECEMBER.

Capricorn, or the horned Goat.

About the twentieth of the month the sun enters this sign: a man born at this time will be of an ambitious, turbulent, and restless disposition, troublesome to himself and others, of a dull and lazy habit, void of reflection, and of unpleasant manners. In life he will be unhappy and unfortunate, owing to his own rashness and want of consideration. In love he will be exceedingly amorous, much attached to the female sex, rather fickle in his affections, but kind and loving to his wife, punctual in the discharge of the nuptial duties; he will make a bad father, but a good husband.

A woman born at this time will be of a meek, sober, and amiable disposition, a good neighbor, and a sincere friend, fearful and timorous, but of engaging manners. In life she will be rather happy than otherwise, and easily restrained from doing wrong. In love she will

be of a warm constitution, and yield easily to the solicitations of her lovers; in the married state she will be faithful and kind, strongly attached to the hymenial duties, and forward in exacting them of her husband; she will be a tender mother and a good wife, though extremely credulous of every thing she hears.

It will be necessary to observe, that the dispositions and events we have mentioned will be more forcible in proportion to the progress the sun has made in the sign; and that they will be considerably altered by a junction of any of the other planets with the sun as their motion is very unequal, we can only lay down the general influence they have, leaving it to the judgment of our readers to apply them: we shall here lay down a plan by which they will be enabled to ascertain what planet was mostly in conjunction with the sun at the time of their birth. When you have ascertained positively the month and the day, examine your own disposition, and that with strict impartiality, neither attributing to yourself virtues you do not possess, nor ascribing to yourself vices to which you are not addicted. Separate all your qualities in your mind, and try which of them has the greatest sway; by these means you will easily discover what planet was predominant at the time of your birth—from what we are going to describe of them and their influence over human nature.

Saturn

Is the most malignant of all the planets, and is thirty years passing through the twelve signs; thus it happens very rarely that the sun enters the same sign with him, at the same time, which is absolutely necessary to give an influence over man. This may be deemed a very fortunate circumstance for mankind, as persons who are born under his influence are morose, sour, tyrannical, cruel, and bloody in their dispositions, given to murder and robbery, in short, worse than savages. Whenever blood is wantonly shed, or murder is attended with any shocking barbarity, you may be well assured that Saturn presided at the birth of those who perpetrated such foul deeds, it being the character of this planet.

Jupiter

Is twenty-three months in performing his revolution through the signs—his conjunction with the sun therefore happens but seldom; those born under this planet are remarkable for their ungovernable ambition, to gratify which they would trample down the lives and fortunes of their fellow-creatures without remorse, and sever the dearest and most tender ties which nature has given to man,

Mars

Is also twenty-three months journeying through the signs—persons born under the influence of this planet which seldom comes in conjunction with the sun, are remarkable for their desire for glory, and the reputation of being courageous. Thus it is that men frequently destroy their fellow-creatures to satisfy their idle appetites, and acquire a reputation for what they falsely conceive to be courage and glory.

Venus

Is the most benignant of all the planets, she presides over and inspires that secret desire, that natural impulse which pervades all creatures to propagate their species, that which nothing can give so sure, so durable, and such frequent transport to the thinking mind; that inspiration to love each other which is found in the sexes, depends entirely on her constant attendance on the sun. Without Venus a tiresome and stupefying apathy would diffuse itself over the whole creation; it is to her benign and maternal influence is owing the exis ence of that desire that constantly urges us to seek in each other the comforts which no individual is capable of finding in himself; and it is her alone that keeps this vivifying spark alive in the human breast. Her mildness restrains and meliorates the rugged suggestions of the other planets; it is thus that frequently we witness the ambitious man losing sight of his object, and retiring to enjoy the exquisite bliss which a judiciously selected female alone can bestow, thus we see the hardy and veteran soldier after the fatigues of battle solacing himself in the embraces of a favorite female companion, thus we see the miser, whose very soul is absorbed in treasure, and who deprives himself of every comfort and necessary of life, under the benign influence of this planet, suffering a beloved woman to bring forth his hoards and unlock those chests that the calls of his own nature, and the distresses of his fellow-creatures, essayed to open in vain—in short, every bliss of which the lover partakes is owing to the influence of this planet, who, happily for mankind, is found frequently in conjunction with the genial sun: Venus may, with great truth be said to light the torch of Hymen.

Mercury

Is equally benignant with Venus, but hath a different influence over man; he is the sun's constant companion and it is to him that we are indebted for wit, memory, understanding, vivacity, and health—but for the predominance of some other planet less favorable to man we should enjoy a state of uninterrupted happiness, be equal in privileges, and be in constant felicity from the influence of this beneficent star.

The Moon

Performs her journey through the signs in about thirty-eight days, when she has the superiority; at the birth of an infant he is dull, inactive, heavy, frigid, insensible to those scenes that take place around him, his blood circulates feebly through his veins, he is a stranger to the joys of love, and nothing but the irresistible power of Venus can arouse him from his lethargy, or set his passions afloat. He is incapable of sincere attachment, and is like a blank in the universe, neither enjoying himself nor promoting the happiness of others.

We shall now present our readers with accurate lists of Lucky and Unlucky Days, with which we shall conclude this division of our labors.

LIST OF UNLUCKY DAYS,

Which, to those Persons being males born on them, will generally prove unfortunate.

January, 3, 4.
February, 6, 7, 12, 13, 19, 20.
March, 5, 6, 12, 13.
May, 12, 13, 20, 21, 26, 27.
June, 1, 2, 9, 10, 16, 17, 22, 23, 24.
July, 3, 4, 10, 11, 16, 17, 18.
October, 3, 4, 9, 10, 11, 16, 17, 31.
November, 1, 3.

Almost all persons (being of the male sex) that are born on the days included in the foregoing table, will, in a greater or less degree suffer, not only by pecuniary embarrassment and losses of property, but will also experience great distress and anxiety of mind, much dissatisfaction, dissension, and unhappiness in their family affairs, much disaffection to each other among the married ones, (indeed few of them can *ever* be happy in the married state,) trouble about their children, daughters forming unfortunate attachments, and a variety of untoward events of other descriptions which our limits do not allow us to particularize. The influence of these days are of a quality and tendency calculated to excite in the minds of persons born on them, an extraordinary itch for speculation, to make changes in their affairs, commence new undertakings of various kinds, but all of them will tend nearly to one point—loss of property and pecuniary embarrassments. Such persons who embark their capital on credit in new concerns or engagements, will be likely to receive checks or interruptions to the progress of their schemes or undertakings. Those, who enter into engagements intended to be permanent, whether purchases, leases, partnerships, or in short any other speculation of a description which cannot readily be transferred; or got rid of will dearly *repent their bargains.*

They will find their affairs from time to time much interrupted and agitated, and experience many disappointments in money matters, trouble through bills, and have need of all their activity and address to prop their declining credit; indeed almost all engagements and affairs that are entered upon by persons born on any of these days will receive some sort of check or obstruction. The greater number of those persons born on these days will be subject to weakness or sprains in the knees and ankles, also diseases and hurts in the legs.

LIST OF UNLUCKY DAYS,

Which to those persons (being females) born on them will generally prove unfortunate.

January, 5, 6, 13, 14, 20, and 21.
February, 2, 3, 9, 10, 16, 17, 22, and 23.
March, 1, 2, 8, 9, 16, 17, 28, and 29.
April, 24 and 25.
May, 1, 2, 9, 17, 22, 29, and 30.
June, 5, 6, 12, 13, 18, and 19.
July, 3 and 4.
September, 9 and 16.
October, 20 and 27.
November, 9, 10, 21, 29, and 30.
December, 6, 14, and 21.

We particularly advise all females born on these days to be extremely cautious of placing their affections too hastily, as they will be subject to *disappointments* and *vexations* in that respect; it will be better for them (in those matters) to be guided by the advice of their friends, rather than by their own feelings, they will be less fortunate in placing their affections, than in any other action of their lives, as many of these marriages will terminate in separations, divorces, &c. Their courtships will end in elopements, seductions, and other ways not necessary of explanation. Our readers must be well aware that affairs of importance begun at inauspicious times, by those who have been born at those periods when the stars shed their malign influence, can seldom, if ever, lead to much good; it is, therefore, that we endeavor to lay before them a correct statement drawn from accurate astrological information, in order that by strict attention and care, they may avoid falling into those perplexing labyrinths from which nothing but that care and attention can save them. The list of days we have above given, will be productive of hasty and clandestine marriages—marriages under untoward circumstances, perplexing attachments, and as a natural consequence, the displeasure of friends,

together with family broils, dissensions, and divisions. We now present our readers with a

LIST OF DAYS

USUALLY CONSIDERED FORTUNATE.

With respect to Courtship, Marriage, and Love affairs in general.—Females that were born on the following days may expect Courtships and prospects of Marriage, and which will have a happy termination.

January, 1, 2, 15, 26, 27, 28.
February, 11, 21, 25, 26.
March, 10, 24.
April, 6, 15, 16, 20, 28.
May, 3, 13, 18, 31.
June, 10, 11, 15, 25, 22.
July, 9, 14, 15, 28.
August, 6, 7, 10, 11, 19, 20, 25.
September, 4, 8, 9, 17, 18, 23.
October, 3, 7, 16, 21, 22.
November, 5, 14, 20.
December, 14, 15, 19, 20, 22, 23, 25.

Although the greater number, or indeed nearly all the ladies that are born on the days stated in the preceding list, will be likely to meet with a *prospect* of marriage, or become engaged in some love affair of *more* than ordinary importance, yet it must not be expected that the *result* will be the same with all of them; with some they will *terminate* in *marriage*—with others in disappointment—and some of them will be in danger of forming *attachments* that may prove of a somewhat *troublesome* description. We shall, therefore, in order to enable our readers to distinguish them, give a comprehensive and useful list, showing which of them will be most likely to marry.

Those born within the limits of the succeeding List of Hours, on any of the preceding days, will be the most likely to *marry*—or will, at least, have *Courtships* that will be likely to have a happy termination.

LIST OF FORTUNATE HOURS.

January 2d.   From 30 minutes past 10 till 15 minutes past 11 in the morning; and from 15 minutes before 9 till 15 minutes before 11 at night.

15th.   From 30 minutes past 9 till 15 minutes past 10 in the morning; and from 30 minutes past 7 till 15 minutes past 11 at night.

26th.   From 30 minutes past 8 till 15 minutes past 9 in the morning; and from 7 till 15 minutes past 10 at night.

February 11th and 12th. From 30 minutes past 7 till 15 minutes past 8 in the morning; and from 15 minutes past 6 till 15 minutes before 9 at night.

21st. From 7 till 15 minutes before 8 in the morning; and from 15 minutes past 5 till 15 minutes before 8 at night.

25th and 26th. From 15 minutes before 7 till 30 minutes past 7 in the morning; and from 15 minutes before 5 till 30 minutes past 7 in the evening.

March 10th. From 5 till 15 minutes before 6 in the morning; and from 4 in the afternoon till 15 minutes before 7 in the evening.

April 6th. From 15 minutes past 4 till 5 in the morning; and from 30 minutes past 2 till 15 minutes past 5 in the afternoon.

20th. From 30 minutes past 3 till 15 minutes past 4 in the morning; and from 30 minutes past 1 till 15 minutes past 4 in the afternoon.

May 3d. From 15 minutes before 3 till 30 minutes past 3 in the morning; and from 15 minutes before 1 till 30 minutes past 3 in the afternoon.

13th. From 2 till 15 minutes before 3 in the morning; and from 12 at noon till 15 minutes before 3 in the afternoon.

18th. From 15 minutes before 1 till 30 minutes past 2 in the morning; and from 15 minutes before 12 at noon till 30 minutes past 2 in the afternoon.

31st. From 15 minutes before 1 till 30 minutes past 1 in the morning; and from 15 minutes past 10 in the morning till 15 minutes before 1 in the afternoon.

June. 10th and 11th. From 15 minutes past 10 till 1 in the afternoon; and from 12 at night till 1 in the morning.

15th. From 10 in the morning till 2 in the afternoon; and from 15 minutes before 12 at night till 15 minutes before 1 in the morning.

25th. From 15 minutes past 9 in the morning till 12 at noon; and from 11 to 12 at night.

29th. From 9 in the morning till 15 minutes before 12 at noon; and from 15 minutes before 11 till 15 minutes before 12 at night.

July 9th. From 15 minutes past 8 till 11 in the morning; and from 10 till 11 at night.

14th and 15th. From 8 till 11 in the morning; and from 10 till 11 at night.

28th. From 7 till 10 in the morning; and from 9 till 10 at night.

August 6th and 7th. From 30 minutes past 6 till 15 minutes past 9 in the morning; and from 15 minutes past 8 till 15 minutes past 9 at night.

10 and 11th. From 15 minutes past 6 till 9 in the morning; and from 8 till 9 in the evening.

19th and 20th. From 30 minutes past 5 till 30 minutes past 8 in the morning; and from 30 minutes past 7 till 30 minutes past 8 in the evening.

25th. From 15 minutes past 5 till 8 in the morning; and from 7 till 8 in the evening.

September 4th. From 15 minutes before 5 till 30 minutes past 7 in the morning; and from 30 minutes past 6 till 30 minutes past 7 in the evening.

8th and 9th. From 30 minutes past 4 till 15 minutes past 7 in the morning; and from 15 minutes past 6 till 15 minutes past 7 in the evening.

17th and 18th. From 5 till 15 minutes before 5 in the morning; and from 15 minutes before 6 till 15 minutes before 7 in the evening.

23d. From 30 minutes past 3 till 30 minutes past 5 in the morning; and from 30 minutes past 5 till 30 minutes past 6 in the evening.

October 3d. From 3 till 15 minutes before 6 in the morning; and from 15 minutes past 4 till 15 minutes past 5 in the afternoon.

7th. From 15 minutes before 3 till 30 minutes past 5 in the morning; and from 30 minutes past 4 till 30 minutes past 5 in the afternoon.

16th. From 2 till 5 in the morning; and from 4 till 5 in the afternoon.

21st and 22d. From 15 minutes before 2 till 30 minutes past 4 in the morning; and from 30 minutes past 3 till 15 minutes past 4 in the afternoon.

November 5th. From 1 till 15 minutes before 4 in the morning; and from 15 minutes before 3 till 15 minutes before 4 in the afternoon.

14th. From 15 minutes past 12 till 3 in the morning; and from 2 till 3 in the afternoon.

20th. From 15 minutes before 12 till 15 minutes past 2 in the morning; and from 15 minutes past 1 till 2 in the afternoon.

December 14th and 15th. From 10 till 30 minutes past 12 in the morning; and from 12 at noon till 15 minutes before 1 in the afternoon.

18th and 19th. From 15 minutes before 10 at night till 15 minutes past 5 in the morning; and from 30 minutes past 11 till 15 minutes past 12 at night.

January 3d. From 30 minutes past 10 till 15 minutes past 11 in the morning; and from 15 minutes before 9 till 15 minutes past 11 at night.

12th and 13th. From 15 minutes past 9 till

10 in the morning; and from 15 minutes before 8 to 30 minutes past 10 at night.

18th. From 9 till 15 minutes before 10 in the morning; and from 15 minutes past 7 till 10 at night.

27th. From 9 till 15 minutes before 10 in the morning; and from 7 till 15 minutes before 10 at night.

February 1st. From 8 till 30 minutes past 8 in the morning; and from 6 till 30 minutes past 8 in the evening.

11th and 12th. From 15 minutes before 8 till 30 minutes past 8 in the morning, and from 15 minutes before 6 till 30 minutes past 8 in the evening.

17th. From 7 till 15 minutes before 8 in the morning; and from 15 minutes past 5 till 8 in the evening.

March 1st. From 30 minutes past 6 till 15 minutes past 7 in the morning; and from 30 minutes past 4 till 15 minutes past 7 in the evening.

16th and 17th. From 30 minutes past 5 till 15 minutes past 6 in the morning; and from 15 minutes before 4 till 30 minutes past 6 in the evening.

19th, 20th, 21st, 22d, 23d, 24th, and 25th. From 30 minutes past 5 till 30 minutes past 6 in the morning; and from 30 minutes past 3 till 15 minutes past 6 in the evening.

26th, 27th, 28th, 29th, and 30th. From 15 minutes past 5 till 15 minutes before 6 in the morning; and from 15 minutes past 3 till 6 in the evening.

April 3d, 4th, 5th, 6th, 7th, 8th, and 9th. From 30 minutes past 4 till 30 minutes past 5 in the morning; and from 30 minutes past 2 till 5 in the afternoon.

10th, 11th, 12th, 13th, and 14th. From 15 minutes before 4 till 15 minutes before 5 in the morning and from 2 till 30 minutes past 4 in the afternoon.

19th, 20th, 21st, 22d, and 23d. From 30 minutes past 4 in the morning; and from 15 minutes before 2 till 30 minutes past 4 in the afternoon.

25th, 26th, 27th, and 28th. From 3 till 4 in the morning; and from 15 minutes past 1 till 15 minutes before 4 in the afternoon.

May 3d, 4th, 5th, 6th, 7th, and 8th. From 15 minutes past two till 15 minutes past 3 in the morning; and from 30 minutes past 12 at noon till 15 minutes past 3 in the afternoon.

9th, 10th, 11th, 12th, and 13th. From 2 till 3 in the morning; and from 15 minutes past 12 at noon till 3 in the afternoon.

16th, 17th, 18th, 19th, 20th, 21st, and 22d. From 15 minutes before 2 till 15 minutes before 3 in the morning; and from 12 at noon till 15 minutes before 3 in the afternoon.

23d, 24th, 25th, 26th, and 27th. From 15 minutes past 1 till 15 minutes past 2 in the morning; and from 30 minutes past 11 in the forenoon till 15 minutes past 2 in the afternoon.

June 1st, 2d, 3d, 4th, 5th, and 6th. From 15 minutes past 10 in the morning till 1 in the afternoon; and from 15 minutes past 12 at night till 15 minutes past 1 the next morning.

11th. From 15 minutes past 10 in the morning till 15 minutes before 1 in the afternoon; and from 12 at night till 1 the next morning.

20th. From 30 minutes past 9 in the morning till 12 at noon; and from 11 till 12 at night.

25th. From 15 minutes past nine in the morning till 15 minutes past 12 at noon; and from 11 till 12 at night.

July 5th. From 15 minutes before 8 till 15 minutes past 10 in the morning; and from 15 minutes before 10 till 15 minutes before 11 at night.

9th. From 15 minutes past 8 till 11 in the morning; and from 15 minutes past 10 till 11 at night.

19th. From 30 minutes past 7 till 10 in the morning; and from 15 minutes past 9 till 15 minutes past 10 at night.

24th. From 7 till 15 minutes before 10 in the morning; and from 9 till 10 at night.

August 2d and 3d. From 30 minutes past 6 till 15 minutes before 9 in the morning; and from 30 minutes past 8 till 30 minutes past 9 at night.

6th. From 15 minutes before 6 till 9 in the morning; and from 30 minutes past 7 till 30 minutes past 8 at night.

22d. From 15 minutes past 5 till 8 in the morning; and from 15 minutes past 7 till 15 minutes past 8 at night.

September 1st. From 4 till 15 minutes before 7 in the morning; and 6 till 7 in the evening.

5th. From 30 minutes past 4 till 15 minutes before 7 in the morning; and from 30 minutes past 6 till 30 minutes past 7 in the evening.

14th. From 15 minutes before 4 till 30 minutes past 6 in the morning; and from 30 minutes past 5 till 30 minutes past 6 in the evening.

29th. From 15 minutes before 3 till 30 minutes past 5 in the morning; and from 30 minutes past 4 till 30 minutes past 5 in the evening.

October 3rd. From 3 till 15 minutes before 6 in the morning; and from 15 minutes before 5 till 15 minutes before 6 in the evening.

12th. From 15 minutes past 2 till 5 in the

morning; and from 15 minutes before 4 till 30 minutes past 4 in the afternoon. 18th and 19th. From 30 minutes past 1 till 4 in the morning; and from 15 minutes before 3 till 30 minutes past 4 in the afternoon.

November 10th and 11th. From 30 minutes past 12 at night till 15 minutes past 3 in the morning; and from 30 minutes past 1 till 30 minutes past 2 in the afternoon.

15th and 16th. From 12 at night till 15 minutes before 3 in the morning; and from 15 minutes past 1 till 2 in the afternoon.

29th and 30th. From 15 minutes past 11 at night till 2 in the morning; and from 1 till 15 minutes before 2 in the afternoon.

December 8th and 9th. From 15 minutes past 10 at night till 1 in the morning; and from 30 minutes past 12 at noon till 30 minutes past 1 in the afternoon.

14th, 15th, and 16th. From 10 at night till 15 minutes before 1 in the morning; and from 15 minutes before 12 till 30 minutes past 12 at noon.

23rd and 24th. From 15 minutes past 11 till 12 at noon, and from 15 minutes past 9 till 12 at night.

28th. From 15 minutes past 10 till 11 in the morning; and from 9 till 15 minutes before 12 at night.

We do not presume to assert that every lady born on the last mentioned times, will be exempt from all descriptions of trouble during the whole of their lives, but that they will never (in spite of whatever may happen to befall them) sink below mediocrity. Even servants and those born of poor parents will possess some superior qualities—get into good company—be much noticed by their superiors, and will, in spite of any intervening difficulties, establish themselves in the world, and rise much above their sphere of birth.

It has often been recorded, and though a singular observation, experience has shown it to be a true one, that some event of importance is sure to happen to a woman in her thirty-first year, whether single or married; it may prove for her good, or it may be some great evil or temptation; therefore we advise her to be cautious and circumspect in all her actions. If she is a maiden or widow, it is probable she will marry this year. If a wife that she will lose her children or her husband:—She will either receive riches or travel into a foreign land: at all events, some circumstance or other will take place during this remarkable year of her life, that will have great effect on her future fortunes and existence.

The like is applicable to men in their forty-second year, of which so many instances have been proved that there is not a doubt of its truth: Observe always to take a lease for an odd number of years; even are not prosperous. —The three first days of the moon are the best for signing papers, and the first five days as well as the twenty-fourth for any fresh undertaking. But we cannot but allow that a great deal depends on our own industry and perseverance, and by strictly discharging our duty to God and man, we may often overcome the malign influence of a bad planet, or a day marked as unlucky in the book of fate.

BOOK THE SECOND.

METRAGRAMMATISM.

Or, the Art of Fortune-Telling by Transposition of Names.

It has often been remarked, although it is a fact by no means commonly known, that the names given to children at the baptismal font joined to their family or surnames, and added to titles which may be bestowed upon them in after-life, often point out many circumstances and events which may befall the parties upon whom such names have been bestowed; and that if their parents had paid more attention to this part of Astrological divination, those names which were unlucky might, by due care and attention, have been avoided, while those of a more fortunate description might have been selected for their children, and have been rendered even still more valuable and fortunate, by being conjoined with others of a like nature. I set order that our readers may have a clearer insight into this branch of fortune-telling, and which appears to have been strangely neglected by modern practitioners, we shall lay before them a few specimens of this admirable system of discovering the events of our checkered existence; and from a study of which they will readily learn how to avoid bestowing on their children such as are of a malignant nature; and, at the same time, perceive how the secret influence of the stars that preside at our birth, act in the minutest manner—even to the giving of that name at our baptism, which oftentimes explains to the bearer of it, if he could then but know it, those events which will assuredly befall him in the course of his life.

Of the antiquity of this science it is scarcely necessary to speak—it may however be as well to remark, that it was formerly in the highest repute among the astrologers of the early ages, and even some of our ancient English writers have not disdained to advocate its cause. One of these, the celebrated Camden, has in his

" *Remains* " bequeath to the world an excellent treatise on this subject. He refers the origin of this invention to the time of Moses, and conceives that it might have had some share in the mystical traditions, afterward called *Cabala*, communicated by that divine lawgiver to the chosen seventy.—That this art was practiced by the ancient Egyptians there cannot be a doubt, as there are even now remaining several of the names of the Egyptian monarchs which have been transposed and fully point out the principal events of their lives. The Greeks also practiced the art, but we do not find any examples among the Romans, which is somewhat surprising, as their seers, astrologers, and sybils practiced almost every species of divination. Among modern nations, the French appear to have distinguished themselves for their proficiency in it, and which, Camden says, " they exceedingly admire and celebrate for the deep antiquity and *mystical meaning* thereof." Indeed, to such a height did that nation carry the practice of this art in the early ages, that there were kept lists of lucky and unlucky names, and particular care was taken, when bestowing a name on a child, that such only should be given as could, by transposition, be formed into some fortunate signification. But this often failed, for even those very names which, when transposed, contained this fortunate signification ; yet, by a second transposition, sometimes quite the contrary would be indicated, and thus

" Foil those, who would have foil'd the stars."

Having thus introduced this subject to our readers, and fully proved its antiquity, it only remains for us to lay before them such specimens of the art, as may enable them to practice upon their own names, and by so doing become acquainted with that principal occurrence of their lives, which may be for their future good or evil ; and if the latter, by possessing such foreknowledge, by caution and good conduct on their parts, alleviate or prevent its affects. We shall take these instances from the names of well known characters, by which it will be instantly seen how immediate is the connection between the name of the party and the principal event of their lives. And first with the name of Bonaparte, which is perhaps the most complete specimen of the art we could possibly lay before our readers, and if properly transposed fully shows in each transposition the character of the man, and points out that unfortunate occurrence in his life, which ultimately proved his ruin—thus

NAPOLEON BONAPARTE.
NO, APPEAR NOT ON ELBA.

In the name of Wellington we find his future glory perfectly prophesied—thus

ARTHUR WELLESLEY, Duke of Wellington.

LET WELL FOILED GAUL secure thy renown.

And the like in that of Nelson,—thus

HORATIO NELSON.
HONOR EST A NILO,

Which in English means " *Honor is to be found at the Nile !* "
In the name of SIR FRANCIS BURDETT, we find   FRANTIC DISTURBERS,

which fully prophesies the busy scenes of popular riot and disturbance in which he would be engaged.
In the name of the late lamented Princess Charlotte, we have another proof of the infallibility of this art—thus

PRINCESS CHARLOTTE AUGUSTA OF WALES, P.
HER AUGUST RACE IS LOST, O ! FATAL NEWS !

The following anagram on JAMES VIth of Scotland, fully proves that his future fortune was predicted at his baptism—thus

CHARLES JAMES STUART
CLAIMS ARTHUR'S SEAT,

and accordingly, on the death of Queen Elizabeth, he became James I. of England, and thereby possessed the throne which the name given him at his birth plainly foretold !
The above will be sufficient to instruct our readers in this very entertaining and infallible mode of discovering future events. It may be necessary to observe, that some names will not easily form into separate words without the addition or subtraction of one or more, letters : this is always allowable,—for instance, K may be substituted for C—I for J—V for U—and *vice versa.*
These specimens will be sufficient to prove the infallibility of this art ; and many of our readers will find, if they transpose the letters of their own names after the same fashion, that their future good or ill fortune will be thereby plainly pointed out.

BOOK THE SECOND.

CHIROMANCY,

Or, the Art of Fortune-Telling by the lines of the hand :—commonly called Palmistry.

The practical part of chiromancy, is that which gathereth probable predictions from lines, the places of the planets in the hand, and from the notes and characters every where pointed and marked out in the hands and fingers. Our readers will therefore be careful to let the following series be duly observed :—

LIST OF THE LINES IN THE HAND.

1.—*Cardiaca*, or the line of life.
2.—*Epatica*, or the liver line; also called the natural mean.
3.—*Sephalica*, or the line of the head and brain.
4.—*Thoralis*, or the table line.
5.—*Restricta*, or the dragon's tail.
6.—*Via Solis*, or the sun's way.
7.—*Via Lactea*, or the milky way.
8.—*Via Saturnia*, or Saturn's way.
9.—*Cingulum Veneris*, or the girdle of Venus.
10.—*Via Martis*, or the way of Mars.
11.—*Mons Veneris*, or the mount of Venus.
12.—*Curca Martis*, or the cave of Mars.
13.—*Mons Jovis*, or Jupiter's mount.
14.—*Mons Saturn*, or Saturn's mount.
15.—*Mons Solis*, or the Sun's mount.
16.—*Locus Lunæ*, or the Moon's place.
17.—*Mons Mercurii*, or the mount of Mercury.
18.—*Mensa*, or the table containing the part of fortune.
19.—*Pollex*, or the thumb.
20.—*Index*, or the fore finger.
21.—*Medius*, or the middle finger.
22.—*Annularis*, or the ring finger.
23.—*Auricularis*, or the little finger.

It has been a question whether we should give judgment by the right hand or by the left, for it is certain, that in one hand the lines and other signatures are very often more manifest, and are thus more plain to be seen and perspicuous than in the other, as well in the hands of gentlemen as ladies.

In consequence of this, many authors have been doubtful as to whether in both sexes the right or left hand is to be taken, or whether the right hand of a gentleman (as some teach,) and the left of a lady only.

To this we answer, that the hand (in both sexes) should be used, which *shows and exhibits the lines thereof most clearly*, and abounds with a series of characters and signs, yet so, as that the other, whose lines *are more obscure, may pay its contribution*. If in both hands they consent, and appear to be fair and comely, they declare a constancy of fortune and health. The cause of which said diversity is this, he who is born in the day time, and hath a masculine planet (the Sun, Saturn, Jupiter or Mars,) lord of his geniture, bears the more remarkable sign in his right hand, especially when the sign ascending is also masculine. The contrary happens to them that are born by by night, as often as a feminine planet predominates, and the sign ascending is also feminine. If both hands agree, it must be, that in a diurnal na-

tivity the feminine planets rule; or that there falls out a mixture of masculine and feminine; so in the nights by the contrary reason, which diversity must necessarily be observed.

I.—OF THE LINE OF LIFE.

This is also called Cardiaca, or the Heart Line.

1. This being broad, of a lively color, and decently drawn in its bounds, without intersections and points, shows the party long lived, and subject but to few diseases.

2. If slender, short, and dissected with obverse little lines; and deformed either by a pale or black color, it presageth weakness of the body, sickness, and a short life.

3. If orderly joined to the natural mean, and beautified in the angle with parallels, or a little across, it argues a good wit, or an evenness of nature.

4. If the same have branches in the upper parts thereof, extending themselves toward the natural mean, it doth signify riches and honor.

5. If these branches be extended toward the restricta, it threatens poverty, deceits, and unfaithfulness of servants.

6. If in this line there be found some confused little lines, like hairs, be assured of diseases, and they to happen in the first age. When they appear below, if towards the cavea, in the middle; if inwards the patica, in the declining age.

7. If this line be any where broken, it threatens extreme danger of life in that part of the age which the place of the breach showeth; for you may find out the dangerous or diseased years of your age : this line being divided into seventy parts, you must begin your number and account from the lower part thereof, near restricta, for the number falling where the branch is, determines the year.

8. If the character of the sun (as commonly it is made by astrologers) be ever found in this line, it presages the loss of an eye ; but if two such characters, the loss of both eyes.

9. A line ascending from the vital, beneath the congress of it and the epatica to the tuberculum of Saturn showeth an envious man, who rejoiceth at another's calamity, the site of others concurring. This also frequently shows a most perilous Saturine disease in that wherein it toucheth the vital, and it is much worse if it cut the same.

10. But such a line passing from the vital to the annular, to the ring finger, promiseth honors to ensue, from or by the means of some famous lady, or to receive some great favor or present from some lady of honor.

11. The vital line being thicker than ordi-

nary at the end under the fore finger, denotes a laborious old age.

12. A line passing through the vital to the cavea of Mars, foretells of wounds and fevers, and also of misfortunes in journeys.

II.—Of the EPATICA, or NATURAL MEAN.

1. This line being straight, continued, and not dissected by obverse little lines, denotes a healthful body.

2. If it be short or broken, and reach not beyond the concave of the hand, it shows diseases and shortness of life.

3. By how much more the same is produced, by so much longer the life may be warranted.

4. If cut at the end thereof by a small intervening line, it threatens poverty in old age.

5. If in the upper part it be distant from the vital by a great space, it shows distemperatures of the heart, as palpitation, syncope, &c.

6. This also shows prodigality, especially if the table be broad.

7. If tortuous (that is, if it wind and turn several ways,) unequal, of a different color, and dissected, it argues an evil constitution of the liver, and thence diseases, proceeding from the weakness thereof: covetousness also, and a depravity both of nature and wit, especially if it be under the region of the middle finger, and approach toward the cardiaca, thereby making a short or narrow triangle.

8. If decently drawn and well colored, it is a sign of a cheerful and ingenious disposition.

9. If it has a sister, it promises inheritances.

10. If continued with some little hard knots, it denotes manslaughters, either perpetuated, or to be committed, according to the number of these said knots.

11. If therein a cross be found under the region of the middle finger, it announces death to be at hand.

12. If it terminates with a fork toward the ferient, it is a sign of depraved wit, of hypocrisy and evil manners.

13. When it tends to the mensa, it is a token of a slanderous and reproachful tongue, and of envy.

14. When it projects a remarkable cleft through the vital to the mons veneris, and the sister of Mars, especially if the same be of a ruddy color, it warns you to be aware of thieves, and also intimates fraud and deceit of enemies.

15. This cleft likewise insinuates a most vehement heat of the liver, proceeding from the rays of Mars; so that the life becomes in danger, seeing that the line of life is dissected.

16. This line having some breach, yet such a one as that, nevertheless it seems to be almost continued, shows that the manner of life will be, or is, already changed; and this in a declining age, if the breach be under the ring finger; but, if under the middle finger, in the strength of years.

III.—OF THE CEPHALICA, OR LINE OF THE BRAIN.

1. This is called the line of the head and brain, which, if (arising from the place in a due proportion) it connects the lines of the liver and heart in a triangular form, have a lively color, and no intersection falling out between, doth declare a man of admirable prudence, and one of no vulgar wit and fortune.

2. By how much more decent the triangle is, so much better shall the temperature, wit, and courage be : but if it be obtuse, it argues an evil disposed nature, and a man that is rude. If no triangle, far worse—a fool, &c., with a short life.

3. The superior being a right angle, or not very acute, foretells the best temperature of the heart; but when it is too acute, especially if it touch the line of life, upon the region of the middle finger, it argues covetness.

4. The left angle, if it be made upon the natural mean in the ferient, and be a right angle, confirms the goodness of the intellect.

5. But when the cephalica projects unequal clefts to the mons lunæ, thereby making unusual characters; in gentlemen it denounces weakness of the brain, and dangerous sea voyages, but in the ladies' hands it shows frequent sorrows of mind, and difficulties in child-bearing.

6. Equal lines (thus projected) presage the contrary in both sexes, viz. in gentlemen, a good composure of the brain, and fortunate voyages by sea : in ladies, cheerfulness and felicity in child-bearing.

7. This one thing is peculiar to the cephalica ; if it project a cleft or a manifest star, upward to the cavea martis, it signifies boldness and courage; but if it let fall the same downward, thefts, &c.

8. The cephalica, joined to the dragon's tail by a remarkable concourse, promises a prudent and joyful old age.

9. The same drawn upward in the shape of a fork, toward the part of fortune, signifies subtlety in managing affairs, and also craftiness either to do good or bad.

10. If in this said fork a mark appears resembling the part of fortune, as it is noted by astrologers, that gives an ansurance of riches and honor to succeed by ingenuity and art.

IV.—OF THE THORAL LINES.

1. This is also called the line of fortune ; it is termed likewise the mensa, because it makes up the table of the hand; which said line, when it is long enough, and without incisures,

argues a due strength in the principal members of man, and also constancy ; the contrary if it be short, crooked, cut or parted.

2. If it terminate under the mount of Saturn, it shows a vain lying fellow.

3. If projecting small branches to the mount of Jupiter, it promises honors.

4. If there it be naked and simple, it is a sign of poverty and want.

5. If cutting the mouth of Jupiter, cruelty of mind and disposition, with excessive wrath.

6. If it projects a breach between the fore and middle finger in a gentleman, it threateneth a wound in his head ; in a lady, danger in child-bearing.

7. Three lines ascending directly upward from this line, viz. one to the space between the middle and fore finger, a second to the space between the middle and ring finger, and a third to the space between the ring and the little finger, argues a contentious person in many respects.

8. A little line only thus drawn to the interval or space between the middle finger and the ring finger, sorrow or labor.

9. If annexed to the natural mean, so that it makes an acute angle, it bringeth sorrow and labor.

10. If the natural mean be wanting, and the thoral annexed to the vital, it threatens decollation, or a deadly wound.

11. If no mensa at all, it shows a man malevolent, contentious, faithless, inconstant, and of base condition.

12. Confused little lines in the mensa, denote sickness ; if under Mercury, in the former part of the age, under the sun, in the prime thereof ; under the middle finger, in old age.

13. When in this line there are certain points observed, they argue strength of the genitals, and burning lust.

V.—Of the CAUDA DRACONIS, or the RESTRICTA, and the Lines arising thence.

1. If this be double or treble, and drawn by a right and continued track, it promiseth a good composure of the body.

2. That line which is nearest the hand, continued, and of a good color, assureth of great riches.

3. But if the same line be cut in the middle, crooked and very pale, it announces debility of body and want of all things.

4. A cross or star upon the restricta, foreshows tranquillity of life in old age.

5. If there be a star, simple or double, or any lines near the tuberculum of the thumb; in ladies they denote misfortune or infamy.

6. A line running from the restricta through the mons veneris, presageth adversities, either by the means of some kindred or a wife.

7. A line extended from the restricta to the

mons lunæ, denotes adversities and private enemies ; if it be crooked, it doubles the evil, and betokeneth perpetual servitude.

8. Such a line also being clear and straight, and reaching so far as the region of the moon, foretells many journeys by sea and land.

9. If it extend to the tuberculum of the fore finger, it informs the gentlemen that he shall live in a foreign country in great estimation.

10. If to the epatica, it argues an honest behavior and prolongeth life.

11. If to the mons solis (be it simple or double,) it shows exceeding good, and enableth to govern or rule in great affairs.

12. By the same reason, if it pass to the mons Mercurii, it betokeneth that the gentleman is of a sufficient capacity for any employment. But, if it reach not the mons Mercurii, but is broken about the middle and end beneath the mons Mercurii, that makes out a prating fellow, a liar, &c.

13. If directly ascending to the mons Saturni, it signifies a good position of Saturn in the geniture, whose decree shall shortly follow. But if crookedly both toward the restricta and the epatica especially, it shows man laborious, &c.

VI.—Of the VIA SOLIS, or the Sun's Way.

This being whole, equally drawn and well colored promiseth the favor of great men and great honors. But if dissected and unequal, the contrary, and exposes to divers impediments, and envy in attaining the same.

VII.—Of the VIA LACTEA, or the Milky Way.

This well proportionate and continued presages that journeys will be fortunate both by sea and by land, a ready wit, and the favor of the ladies (Venus assenting,) of a composed and graceful speech ; but if it be cut or distorted, it argues infelicity and lies : but whole and ascending to the little finger, it is a sign of great happiness.

VIII.—Of the SATURNIA, or the Line of Saturn.

1. This being fully and wholly protracted to the middle finger, is an argument both of profound cogitations, and likewise of fortunate events in counsels and actions.

2. Combust or deficient, an evil sign portending many misfortunes, unless either positions favor it.

3. Bending backward in the cavea of the hand, toward the ferient, in the form of a semi-circle, threatens imprisonment.

4. A line drawn from the vital through the epatica to the tuberculum of Saturn (if it touch the Saturnia,) the same.

IX.—Of the CINGULUM VENERIS, or the Girdle of Venus.

If this line have a sister, it argues intemperance and lust in both sexes, and baseness in venereal congressions, a filthy man, especially who abhors not an abominable unnatural crime; and, if dissected and troubled, it shows losses and infamy by reason of lusts.

X.—Of the VIA MARTIS, the Way or Line of Mars, or the Vital Sister.

This fine (as often as it appeareth) augments and strengthens the things signified by the cardiaca, but particularly, it promises good success in war, provided it be clear and red.

Some Observations concerning Lines.

1. The quantity of all lines must be wisely observed, that is, the length and depth; so likewise their quality, that is, their complexion and shape, whether they are crooked or straight; next their action, which is to touch or cut other lines. Their passion to be touched or cut of others; and, lastly, their place and position.

2. We must know, that the lines are sometimes prolonged until certain years of our age, otherwise shortened; now they wax pale, then they become plain and strong, and as it were luxuriate with a kind of redness, and this as well in the principal as less principal lines. Again, as touching the less principal, and such as are found in the tubercula of the planets, it is most certain, that some do one time quite vanish, and that at another time others arise of a different shape and complexion; the cause of which, I suppose to be no other than the various progressions of the alphabetical places in their nativities; that is to say, fortunate and unfortunate, to the influence whereof man himself is wonderfully subject. The signs of his hand are presented at different times with quite different faces. *Such a virtue, such a love, resideth in the imagination of the greater world toward the lesser.* And therefore, the most studious in chiromancy cannot attain the knowledge of particulars by one inspection only, made to a certain year of the person's age; things that worthily merit our observations, yet known or approved of but by a few.

XI.—The MENSA, or part of FORTUNE.

1. This space being great and broad, and the figure decent, declares a liberal man, magnanimous, and of a long life.

2. But if small and narrow, it indicates a slender fortune and fearfulness.

3. A cross or star within it, clear and well proportioned especially under the region of the ring finger, betokeneth honors and dignities to ensue from, or by means of great and noble personages. If the character of Jupiter, it then promises great ecclesiastical dignities, &c.

4. The same star or cross tripled, excellently increaseth portents of good fortune; but if it be cut by confused little lines, the good fortune is thereby diverted, and anxieties and labors threatened in defending his honors, especially if they are under the region of the ring finger.

5. A cross or star in the uppermost part of the mensa, is a sign of fortunate journeys.

6. The mensa sharpened by the concourse of the thoral and cardiac lines, point out deceits and danger of life.

7. If no mensa be found in the hand, it shows obscurity both of life and fortune.

8. Good and equal lines in this space do declare the fortune to be good, but if evil and discomposed they quite overthrow it.

9. A little circle shows perfection of wit, and the obtaining of sciences, the others assenting thereunto.

XII.—Of the FINGERS,—The POLLEX, or Thumb.

Overthwart lines, that are clear and long underneath the nail and joint of the thumb, confer riches and honor. A line passing from the upper joint of the thumb to the cardiaca, threatens a violent death, or danger, by means of some married lady. Lines every where dispersed in the lower joint of the thumb, describe men that are contentious, and such as rejoice in scolding, &c. A line surrounding the thumb in the middle joint, portends the man shall be hanged. Equal furrows drawn under the lower joint thereof, argue riches and possessions. If the first or second joint want incisures, it shows drowsiness and idleness.

XIII.—The INDEX, or Fore Finger.

Many lines in the uppermost joint and they proceeding overthwartly, denote inheritances; by running so in the middle joint, an envious and evil disposed person.

Right lines running between these joints, declare (in the ladies) a numerous issue. In gentlemen, bitterness of the tonge. If they are in the first joint near unto Jupiter's mouth, they manifest a jovial disposition, that is they point to the man whom Jupiter favored well in his nativity. That woman who hath a star in the same place, may safely be pronounced unchaste and lascivious.

XIV.—MEDIUS, or the Middle Finger.

This finger presenting little gridirons in the joints thereof, plainly declares an unhappy and melancholy wit, but if equal lines, it manifesteth fortune by metals, &c. A star there presages a violent death by drowning, &c. If a cross line be extended from the root thereof upward, through the whole finger into the end of the last joint it argues folly and madness.

XV.—ANNULARIS, or the Ring Finger.

A line arising from mons solis, and ascending by a right track through the joints thereof, it shows a noble frame. Equal lines in the first joint demonstrates honor and riches. Overthwart lines, the enmity of great men. Howbeit, if these lines shall seem to be intersected, it is the better, because they argue impediments.

XVI.—AURICULARIS, or the Little Finger.

From the joint thereof, as from the mount itself are judgments and decrees passed concerning merchandize, favors, and a star in the first joint near the tuberculum, argues ingenuity and eloquence.

Other obtuse signs the contrary; but when there appear unfortunate signs in the first and second joints, they mark out a thief and a very deceitful person. If adverse lines in the last joint, perpetual inconstancy.

Some there are who predict the number of wives from the little lines in the mons Mercurii at the outmost part of the hand, and I have often observed them come at the truth; but yet I will not confirm any thing in this respect, because it properly appertains to Venus and her disposition.

If the end of this finger reach not so far as to touch the last joint of the ring finger, it signifies a wife most imperious in all things, the truth thereof is often proved.

Observations on the Fingers.

The structure of the hand itself is most admirable in respect to the proportion it beareth to the face, and certain parts thereof, which is this:—

1. The whole hand is of equal length with the face.

2. The greater joint of the fore finger equals the height of the forehead.

3. The other two (to the extremity of the nail) is just the length of the nose, viz. from the intercelia, or place between the eyebrows to the tip of the nostrils.

4. The first and greater joint of the middle finger, is just as long as it is between the bottom of the chin, and the top of the under lip.

5. But the third joint of the same finger is of equal length, with the distance that is between the mouth and the lower part of the nostrils.

6. The largest joint of the thumb gives the width of the mouth.

7. The distance between the bottom of the chin, and the top of the lower lip, the same.

8. The lesser joint of the thumb is equal to the distance between the top of the under lip, and the lower part of the nostrils. The nails obtain just the half of their respective uppermost joints, which they call omychios.

BOOK THE FOURTH.

NÆVIOLOGY,

Or, the Science of foretelling future events by Moles, Marks, Scars, or other signs on the skin. Showing their situation, and by that the indication they give of a person's disposition and future lot in life.

THESE little marks on the skin; although they appear to be the effect of chance, or accident, and might easily pass with the unthinking for things of no moment, are nevertheless of the utmost consequence, since from their color, situation, size, and figure, may be accurately gathered the temper of, and the events that will happen to the person bearing them; though moles are, in their substances, nothing else than excrescences, or ebullitions which proceed from the, state of the blood whilst the fœtus is confined in the womb, yet they are not given in vain, as they are generally characteristic of the disposition and temper of those that bear them; and it is also proved by daily experience, that from the shape, situation, and other circumstances, they bear a strong analogy to the events which are to happen to a person in future life. But before I presume to give any directions to those who are to form the prognostic, who are desirious to be duly enabled to pronounce an infallible judgment, I shall, in the first place, teach you herein the common prognostications by moles found in the various parts of the body, according to the doctrine of the ancients. And, first it is essentially necessary to know the size of the mole, its color, whether it be perfectly round, oblong, or angular; because each of these will add to or diminish the force of the indication. The larger the mole, the greater will be the prosperity or adversity of the person; the smaller the mole, the less will be his good or evil fate. If the mole is round, it indicates good; if oblong, a moderate share of fortunate events; if angular, it gives a mixture of good and evil; the deeper the color, the more it announces favor or disgrace; the lighter, the less of either. If it is very hairy, much misfortune may be expected; if but few long hairs grow upon it, it denotes that your undertakings will be prosperous.

We shall further remark only, that moles of a middling size and color are those which we are now going to speak of. The rest may be gathered from what we have just above mentioned, but as it may frequently happen that modesty will sometimes hinder persons from showing their moles, you must depend upon their own representation of them for your opinion.

On the Wrist, or between that and the Finger ends,

Shows the person to be of an ingenious and industrious turn, faithful in his engagements, amorous and constant in his affections, rather of a saving disposition, with a great degree of sobriety and regularity in his dealing. It foreshows a comfortable acquisition of fortune, with a good partner, and beautiful children, but some disagreeable circumstances will happen about the age of thirty, which continue four of five years. In a man, it denotes being twice married—in a woman only once, but that she will survive her husband.

Between the Elbow and the Wrist.

Shows a placid and cheerful disposition, industry, and a love of reading, particularly books of science,—it foretells much prosperity and happiness toward the middle of life, but after having undergone many hardships, if not imprisonment—it also denotes that your eldest son will rise to honors in the state, and marry a woman not of his own country, who will bring him much riches.

Near either Elbow,

Shows a restless and unsteady disposition, with a great desire of traveling—much discontented in the married state, and of an idle turn—it indicates no very great prosperity, rather a sinking than rising condition, with many unpleasant adventures, much to your discredit—marriage, to a person who will make you unhappy, and children who will be disobedient, and cause you much trouble.

On the right or left Arm,

Shows a courteous disposition, great fortitude, resolution, industry, and conjugal fidelity—it foretells that the person will fight many battles, and be successful in all; that you will be prosperous in your undertakings, obtain a decent competency, and live very happy—it denotes that a man will be a widower at forty, but in a woman it shows that she will be survived by her husband.

On the left Shoulder,

Shows a person of a quarrelsome and unruly disposition, always inclined to dispute for trifles, rather indolent, but much inclined to the pleasures of love, and faithful to the conjugal vows. It denotes a life much varied either with pleasures or misfortunes—they indicate many children, and moderate success in business, but dangers by sea.

On the right Shoulder,

Shows a person of a prudent and discreet temper, one possessed of much wisdom, given to great secrecy, very industrious, but not very amorous, yet faithful to conjugal ties—it indicates great prosperity and advancement in life, a good partner, and many friends, with great profit from a journey to a distant country, about the age of thirty-five.

On any part from the Shoulders to the Loins,

Shows and even and mild temper, given to sloth, and rather cowardly, very amorous, but unfaithful—it denotes decay in health and wealth, with troubles and difficulties in the decline of life, and much vexation from children.

On the Loins,

Shows industry and honesty, an amorous disposition, with great vigor, courage, and fidelity—it foretells success in business, and in love, many children, acquirement of riches and honor, with much traveling—it also indicates a great loss by lending of money, and quarrelling among friends, who will attempt to decieve you.

On either Hip,

Shows a contented disposition, given to industry, amorous and faithful in engagements, of an abstemious turn—it foretells moderate success in life, with many children, who will undergo many hardships with great fortitude, and arrive at ease and affluence by dint of their industry and ingenuity.

On the right Thigh,

Shows the person to be of an agreeable temper, inclined to be amorous, and very courageous—it also denotes success in life, accumulation of riches by marriage, and many fine children, chiefly girls.

On the left Thigh.

Shows a good and benevolent disposition, a great turn for industry, and little inclined to the pleasures of love—it indicates many sorrows in life, great poverty, unfaithful friends, and imprisonment by false swearing.

On the left Knee,

Shows a hasty and passionate disposition, extravagant and inconsiderate turn, with no great inclination to industry and honesty, much given to the pleasures of Venus, but possessed of much benevolence—it indicates good success in undertakings, particularly in contracts, a rich marriage, and an only child.

On the right Knee,

Shows an amiable temper, honest disposition, and a turn for amorous pleasures and industry —it foretells great success in love, and the choice of a conjugal partner, with few sorrows, many friends, and dutiful children.

On either Leg.

Shows a person of a thoughtless, indolent disposition, of an amorous turn, much given to extravagance and dissipation—it denotes many difficulties through life, but that you will surmount them all—it shows that imprisonment will happen to you at an early age, but that in general you will be more fortunate than otherwise ; you will marry an agreeable person, who will survive you, by whom you will have four children, two of which will die young.

On either Ankle,

Shows an effeminate disposition, given to foppery in dress, and cowardice in a man ; but in a woman it denotes courage, wit, and activity— they foretell success in life with an agreeable partner, accumulation of honors and riches and much pleasure in the affairs of love.

On either Foot,

Shows a melancholy and inactive disposition, little inclined to the pleasures of love, given to reading and a sedentary life—they foretell sickness, and unexpected misfortunes, with many sorrows and much trouble, an unhappy choice of a partner for life, with disobedient and unfortunate children.

On the right side of the Forehead, or right Temple,

Shows an active and industrious disposition, much given to the sports of love—it denotes that she will be very successful in life, marry an agreeable partner, and arrive at unexpected riches and honors, and have a son, who will become a great man.

On the right Eyebrow,

Shows a sprightly active disposition, a great turn for gallantry, much courage, and great perseverance—it denotes wealth, and success in love, war, and business ; that you will marry an agreeable mate, live happy, have children, and die in an advanced old age, at a distance from home.

On the left Eyebrow, Temple, or side of the Forehead.

Shows an indolent, peevish temper, a turn for debauchery and liquor, little inclined to amorous sports, and very cowardly—it foretells poverty, imprisonment, and disappointments in all your undertakings, with undutiful children, and a bad tempered partner.

On the outside corner of either Eye,

Shows a sober, honest, and steady disposition, much inclined to the pleasures of love—it foretells a violent death, after a life considerably varied by pleasures and misfortunes—in general it foreshows that poverty will keep at a distance.

On either Cheek,

Shows an industrious, benevolent, and sober disposition, given to be grave and solemn, little inclined to amorous sports, but of a steady courage and unshaken fortitude—it denotes a moderate success in life, neither becoming rich nor falling into poverty—it also foretells an agreeable and industrious partner, with two children, who will do better than the parents.

On the Chin,

Shows an amiable and tranquil disposition, industrious and much inclined to traveling, and the joys of Venus—it denotes that the person will be highly successful in life, accumulating a large and splendid fortune, with many respectable and worthy friends, an agreeable conjugal partner, and fine children—but also indicates losses by sea and in foreign countries.

On either Lip,

Shows a delicate appetite, a sober disposition, and much given to the pleasures of love, of an industrious and benevolent turn—it denotes that the person will be successful in undertakings, particularly in love affairs—that you will rise above your present condition, and be greatly respected and esteemed, that you will endeavor to obtain some situation, in which you will at first prove unsuccessful, but afterward prevail.

On the Nose,

Shows a hasty and passionate disposition, much given to amorous pleasures, faithful to engagements, candid, open, and sincere in friendship, courageous and honest, but very petulant, and rather given to drink—it denotes great success through life and in love affairs, that you will become rich, marry well, have fine children, and be much esteemed by your neighbors and acquaintance—that you will travel much, particularly by water.

On the Throat,

Shows a friendly and generous disposition, of a sober turn, given to industry, extremely amorous, and much inclined to indulge in the joys of Venus—it denotes riches by marriage, and great success afterward in your undertakings, with fine children, who will go to a far distant country, where they will marry, grow rich, and return to their native land.

On the side of the Neck,

Shows a meek and sober disposition, moderately inclined to the pleasures of love, but firm and steady in friendship, rather given to industry—it denotes much sickness, and that you will be in great danger of suffocation, but that you will rise to unexpected honors and dignity, receive large legacies, and grow very rich—but also that your children will fall into poverty and disgrace.

On the right Breast,

Shows an intemperate and indolent disposition, rather given to drink, strongly attached to the joys of love—it denotes much misfortune in life, with a sudden reverse from riches to poverty—many unpleasant and disagreeable accidents, with a sober and industrious partner—many children, mostly girls, who will all marry well, and be a great comfort to your old age—it warns you to beware of pretended friends, who will harm you much.

On the left Breast,

Shows an industrious and sober disposition, amorous, and much given to walking—it denotes great success in life and in love, that you will accumulate riches, and have many children, mostly boys, who will make their fortunes by sea.

On the Bosom,

Shows a quarrelsome and unhappy temper, given to low debauchery, and exceedingly amorous, indolent and unsteady—it denotes a life neither very prosperous nor very miserable, but passed without many friends or much esteem.

Under the left Breast over the Heart,

Shows a rambling unsettled disposition, given to drinking and little careful of your actions: very amorous, and much given to indulge indiscriminately in the pleasures of love, in a man. In a woman it indicates sincerity in love, industry, and a strict regard for character—in life it denotes a varied mixture of good and bad fortune, the former rather prevailing—it denotes

imprisonment for debt, but not of long duration. To a woman it denotes easy labors, and children who will become rich, live happy and respected, and marry well.

On the right Side near any part of the Ribs,

Shows an indolent cowardly disposition, given to excessive drinking, of an inferior capacity, and little inclined to the pleasures of love—it denotes an easy life, rather of poverty than riches, little respected, a partner of an uneven and disagreeable temper, with undutiful children, who will fall into many difficulties.

On the Belly,

Shows an indolent slothful disposition, given to gluttony, very selfish, addicted to the pleasures of love and drink, negligent of dress, and cowardly—it denotes small success in life, many crosses, some imprisonment, and traveling, with losses by sea; but it foretells that you will marry an agreeable partner of a sweet temper, have children who will be industrious and become very respectable in life.

On the Privy Members, or parts,

Shows a generous, open and honest disposition, extremely disposed to gallantry, and the joys of Venus, given to sobriety, and of undaunted courage—it denotes great success in the latter part of life, but many and severe misfortunes in the former, which will be borne with fortitude—it also foretells a happy marriage and fine children, who will be happy, thrive well and grow rich and respectable—in man it shows that he will have natural children, who will cut a great figure in life, but he will experience much plague and vexation from their mother.

BOOK THE FIFTH.

PHYSIOGNOMY.

Or, Prognostics drawn from the Color and Nature of the Hair of Men and Women, as also from the Forehead, Eyebrows, Eyes, Nose, Mouth, Chin, and whole assemblage of Features.

1. The gentleman whose hair is very black and smooth, hanging far over his shoulders; and in large quantity, is mild but resolute; cool, until greatly provoked; not much inclined to excess of any kind, but may be persuaded to it. He is constant in his attachment, and not liable to many misfortunes.

2. A lady, of the same kind of hair, is moderate in her desires of every kind, addicted to

reflection, and though not subject to violence in love, is steady in her attachments, and no enemy to its pleasures; of a constitution neither vigorous nor yet feeble.

3. If the hair is very black, short, and curling, the gentleman will be given to liquor, somewhat quarrelsome, and of an unsettled temper, more amorous, and less steady in his undertakings, but ardent at the beginning of an enterprise. He will be very desirous of riches, but will often be disappointed in his wishes therein.

4. The same may be said of a lady.

5. A gentleman with dark brown, long, and smooth hair, is generally of a robust constitution, obstinate in his temper, eager in his pursuits, a lover of the fair sex, fond of variety, in his ordinary pursuits exceedingly curious, and of a flexible disposition. He will live long, unless guilty of early intemperance.

6. A lady of the same kind of hair will be nearly the same as the gentleman, but more steady in her conduct and attachments, especially in love. She will be of a good constitution, have many children, be much respected, enjoy good health, and a reasonable share of happiness.

7. If the hair is short and bushy, it will make very little alteration in the gentleman or lady, but that the gentleman will be more forward to strike when provoked, and the lady will be more of a scold.

8. A gentleman with light brown long smooth hair, is of a peaceable, even, and rather, a generous temper; will prevent mischief if in his power, but when very much provoked will strike furiously; but is afterward sorry for his passion and soon appeased; strongly attached to the company of the ladies, and will protect them from any insult. Upon the whole, he is in general an amiable character, affable and kind.

9. A lady of the same kind of hair, is tender-hearted, but hasty in temper; neither obstinate nor haughty; her inclinations to love never unreasonable; her constitution will be good, but she will be seldom very fortunate. If the hair is short and bushy, or apt to curl by nature, the gentleman will be more industrious and the lady more sedentary.

10. A gentleman with fair hair will be of a weak constitution; his mind given much to reflection, especially in religious matters. He will be assiduous in his occupation, but not given to rambling; very moderate in his amorous wishes, but not live to an old age.

11. A lady of this colored hair is on the contrary of a good constitution; never to be diverted from her purposes; very passionate in love affairs, never easy unless when in company, and delights in hearing herself praised, especially for beauty; delights in dancing and strong exercises, and commonly lives a great age.

12. A gentleman with long red hair is cunning, artful and deceitful; he is very much addicted to traffic of some kind, restless in his disposition, constantly roving, and desirous of enjoying the pleasures of love. He is covetous of getting money, though he often spends it foolishly; he is indefatigable, and no obstacle will induce him to forsake his enterprise until he has seen the issue of it. He is inclined to timidity, but by reflection may correct it, and pass for a man of courage.

13. A lady of the same kind of hair, is glib of tongue, having words at will, talkative and vain; her temper is impatient and fiery, and will not submit to contradiction; she has a constant flow of spirits, and much given to the pleasures of love. However delicate her person may seem, her constitution is generally vigorous; but she seldom lives to see old age, for very obvious reasons; her promises are seldom to be depended upon, because the next object that engrosses her attention makes her forgetful of every thing that preceded it, and will always resent any disappointment she may meet with.

I will now proceed to give some few instructions concerning the hair in other particulars, by the following remarks:—

14. If the hair falls off at the fore part of the head, the person will be easily led, though otherwise rational, and will often find himself duped, when he thinks he is acting right; he will likewise frequently meet with disappointments in money matters, which will either hurt his credit, or force him to shorten his expenses.

15. If the hair falls off behind, he will be obstinate, peevish, passionate, and fond of commanding others, though he has no right, and will grow angry if his advice is not followed. However preposterous, he will be fond of hearing and telling old stories, and tales of ghosts, goblins, fairies; but will be a good domestic man, and provide for his family to the utmost of his power.

16. If the hair forms an arch round the forehead, without being much indented at the temples, both the gentleman and the lady will be innocent, credulous, peaceable, moderate in all their desires, and though not ardent in their pursuits, will still be persevering. They will be mild, moderate, good-natured, prosperous and happy.

17. If the hair is indented at the temples, the person will be affable, steady, good-natured, prudent, and attentive to business, of a solid constitution, and long lived.

18. If the hair descends low upon the forehead, the person will be selfish and designing; of a surly disposition, unsociable, and given to drinking. He will also be addicted to avarice,

and his mind will be always intent upon the means of carrying on his schemes, &c.

19. The forehead that is large, round, and smooth, announces the lady or gentleman to be frank, open, generous, and free, good-natured, and a safe companion; of a good understanding, and scorns to be guilty of any mean actions; faithful to his promises, just in his dealings, steadfast to his engagements and sincere in his affections; he will enjoy a moderate state of health, &c.

20. If the forehead is flat in the middle, the gentleman or lady will be found to be vainglorious, and but little disposed to generosity; very tenacious of his honor, but brave; he will be fond of prying into the secrets of others, though not with an intention of betraying them; he will be fond of reading newspapers, history, novels, and plays; ardent, and very cautious of his own reputation, &c.

21. If there is a hollow across the forehead, in the middle, with a ridge as of flesh above, and another below, the gentleman will be a good scholar, the lady a great manufacturer, or attentive to whatever occupation she may be engaged in. They will be warm in argument or debate—they will be firm and steady in any point they fix their minds upon, and by their perseverance will generally carry their object, yet they will meet with many crosses, but will bear them with patience.

22. If the forehead jut out immediately at and over the eyebrows, running flat up to the hair, the gentleman or lady will be sullen, proud, insolent, imperious, and treacherous; they will be impatient when contradicted, apt to give great abuse, and to strike if they think they can do it with advantage. They will also impose upon any person, never forgiving an injury, and by their misconduct make themselves many enemies.

23. If their temples are hollow, with the bones advancing toward the forehead on either side, so that the space between must be necessarily flat, with a small channel or indenture rising from the upper part of the nose to the hair, the gentleman or lady will be of a daring and intrepid temper, introducing themselves into matters wherein they have no business, desirous of passing for wits, and of a subtle and enterprising nature; greedy of praise, quick in quarrel, and of a wandering disposition; very lewd, and full of resentment when they feel their pride hurt. In short, they delight in mischief, riots, &c.

24. If the eyebrows are very hairy, and that hair long and curled, with several of the hairs starting out, the gentleman or lady is of a gloomy disposition, litigious, and quarrelsome, although a coward; greedy after the affairs of this world, perpetually brooding over some melancholy subject, and not an agreeable companion. He will be diffident, penurious, and weak in his understanding; never addicted to any kind of learning. He will pretend much friendship, but will make his affected passion subservient to his pecuniary designs, and also given to drinking, &c., &c.

25. If a gentleman or lady has long eyebrows, with some long hairs, they will be of a fickle disposition, weak-minded, credulous, and vain, always seeking after novelties, and neglecting their own business; they will be talkative, pert, and disagreeable in company; very fond of contradiction, but will not bear disappointment patiently; and will also be much addicted to drinking, &c.

26. If the eyebrows are thick and even, that is, without any or few starting hairs, the gentleman or lady will be of an agreeable temper, sound understanding, and tolerable wit; moderately addicted to pleasure, fearful of giving offence, but intrepid and persevering in support of right; charitable and generous, sincere in their professions of love and friendship, and enjoy a good constitution.

27. If the eyebrow is small, thin of hair, and even, the gentleman or lady will be weakminded, timorous, superficial, and not to be depended on; they will be desirous of knowledge, but will not have patience and assiduity enough to give it the necessary attention; they will be desirous of praise for worthy actions, but will not have spirit or perseverance enough to perform them, in that degree of excellence that is requisite to attract the notice of wise men. They will be of a delicate constitution, &c.

28. If the eyebrow is thick of hair toward the nose, and goes off suddenly very thin, ending in a point, the gentleman or lady will be surly, captious, jealous, fretful, and easily provoked to rage; in their love they will be intemperate.

29. The eye that is large, full, prominent, and clear, denotes a gentleman or lady to be of an ingenuous and candid disposition, void of deceit, and of an even, agreeable, and affable disposition; modest and bashful in love, though by no means an enemy to its gratification; firm, though not obstinate; of a good understanding, of an agreeable but not brilliant wit; but clear and just in argument, inclined to extravagance, and easily imposed upon.

30. The eye that is small, but advanced in the head shows the gentleman or lady to be of a quick wit, sound constitution, lively genius, agreeable company and conversation, good morals, but rather inclined to jealousy: attentive to business, fond of frequently changing his place, punctual in fulfilling his engagements, warm in love, prosperous in his undertakings, and generally fortunate in most things.

31. The gentleman or lady whose eyes are sunk in the head, is of a jealous, distrustful,

malicious, and envious nature. deceitful in their words and actions, never to be depended upon; cunning in over reaching others, vain-glorious, and associates with lewd and bad company, &c.

32. The gentleman or lady who squints, or have their eyes turned awry, will be of a penurious disposition, but punctual in their dealings.

33. A black eye is lively, brisk, and penetrating, and proves the person who possesses it to be a sprightly wit, lively conversation, not easily imposed upon, of a sound understanding, but if taken on the weak side, may be led astray for awhile.

34. A hazel eye shows the person to be of a subtle, piercing, and frolicsome disposition, rather inclined to be arch, and sometimes mischievous, but good-natured at the bottom. He will be strongly inclined to love, and not ever delicate in the means of gratifying that propensity.

35. A blue eye shows the person to be of a meek and gentle temper, affable and good-natured, credulous, and incapable of violent attachments; ever modest, cool, and undisturbed by turbulent passions, of a strong memory, in constitution neither robust nor delicate, subject to no violent impressions from the vicissitudes of life, whether good or bad.

36. A grey eye denotes the person to be of weak intellects, devoid of wit, but a plain, plodding, downright drudge, that will act as he is spirited up by others. He will be slow in learning anything that requires attention, however, he will be just to the best of his understanding.

37. A wall eye denotes the person to be a hasty, passionate, and ungovernable temper, subject to sudden and violent anger; haughty to his equals and superiors, but mild and affable to his inferiors.

38. A red, or as it is vulgarly called, a saucer eye, denotes the person to be selfish, deceitful, and proud, and furious in anger, fertile in the invention of plots, and indefatigable in his resolution to bring them to bear. Imperious in his family, anxious for riches, and suspicious that others are forming designs against him, is ardent in love, but strongly attached to the first object that catches his fancy.

39. A nose that comes even on the ridge, flat on the sides, with little or no hollow between the eyes, declares the man to be sulky, insolent, disdainful, treacherous, and self-sufficient; if it has a point descending over the nostrils, he is avaricious and unfeeling, vainglorious and ignorant; peevish, jealous, quick in resentment, yet a coward at the bottom.

40. A nose that rises with a sudden bulge a little below the eyes, and then falls again into a kind of hollow below, is petulant and noisy,

void of science, and of a very light understanding.

41. The nose that is small, slender, and peaked, shows the person to be of a fearful disposition, jealous, fretful, and insidious, ever suspicious of those about him, catching at every word that he can interpret to his own advantage to ground his dispute upon, and also very curious to know what is said and done.

42. The nose that is small, tapering round in the nostrils, and cocked up, shows the person to be ingenuous, smart, of a quick apprehension, giddy, and seldom looking into consequences. but generous, agreeable, so as to carefully avoid giving offence; but firm and resolute in doing justice when he receives an injury.

43. The lips that are thick, soft, and long, announces the person to be of weak intellects, credulous, and slightly peevish; but by little soothing easily brought back to a good humor. He is much addicted to the pleasures of love, and scarcely moderate in his enjoyment of them, yet he is invariably upright in his conduct, and of a timorous bashful temper.

44. If the under lip is much thicker than the upper and more prominent, the person is of a weak understanding, but artful, knavish, and given to chicanery to the full extent of his ability. He is of a cowardly nature, unless strongly excited by another.

45. The lips that are moderately plump and even, declare the person to be good-humored, humane, sensible, judicious, and just, neither giddy nor torpid, but pursuing in every particular a just medium.

46. The lips that are thin, show the person to be of a quick and lively imagination, ardent in the pursuit of knowledge, indefatigable in labor, not too much attached to money, eager in the pursuit of love, more brave than otherwise, and tolerably happy in life.

47. The lips that are thin and sunk inwards, denote the person to be of a subtle and persevering disposition, everlasting in hatred, and never sparing any pains to compass his revenge; in love or friendship much more moderate and uncertain.

48. The chin that is round, with hollow between it and the lip shows the person to be of a good-humored disposition kind and honest; he is sincere in his friendship, and ardent in his love; his understanding is good, and his genius capacious. If he has a dimple it makes him better.

49. The chin that comes down flat from the edge of the lip, ends in a kind of chisel-form, shows the person to be silly, credulous, illtempered, and greedy of unmerited honors, capricious, wavering and unsteady; he will affect great modesty in the presence of others, though he will not scruple to do the vilest actions, when he thinks himself secure from discovery. A dimple makes no alteration.

50. The chin that is pointed upward; shows the person to be much given to contrivances. However fair he may speak to you, you can never depend on his friendship, as his purpose is only to make you subservient to his own designs. In love his generosity will be of the same stamp.

51. Of the face in general, I shall say, that the person whose features are strong, coarse, and unpleasant to the eye, is of a selfish, brutal, rough, and unsocial disposition; greedy of money, harsh in expression, but will sometimes fawn with a bad grace to gain his ends.

52. The face that is plump, round, and ruddy, denotes the person to be of an agreeable temper, a safe companion, hearty and jovial, fond of company, of sound principles and a clear understanding, faithful in love, &c.

53. The face that is thin, smooth, and even, with well-proportioned, features, shows the person to be of a good disposition, but lively, penetrating, and active; somewhat inclined to suspicion, yet of an agreeable conversation; assiduous in the pursuits of knowledge, and strongly addicted to the delights of love.

54. A face whose cheek bones jut out with thin jaws, is of a restless and thinking disposition; fretful, and apprehensive of what may happen on the slightest cause, or what may never happen at all; always foreboding evil without any plausible reason for such fears; more disposed than capable of enjoying the pleasures of love.

55. A face that is pale by nature, denotes a timorous disposition, but greatly desirous of the pleasures of love.

56. A face that is unequally red, whether streaked or appearing in spots, shows the person to be weak both in mind and body, yielding easily to affliction and sickness.

57. A face blotched, shows, the person to be addicted to drinking and vice, and not even free from any vice, though they have frequently the art to conceal the inclination.

58. The head that is large and round, shows that the person has tolerable understanding, but not near so good as he imagines; however, upon the whole, he is rather harmless, and not so much given to vice.

59. The head that is small and round, or if the face comes tapering, shows the person of acute, penetrating disposition, much given to bantering and humor, but of very great sensibility; sometimes hurried by caprice, but commonly faithful in love.

60. The head that is flat on either side and deep from the face to the back, shows the person to be of a good understanding, deep penetration, great memory, and of an even and agreeable temper, but slow of belief, and not easily imposed upon. He is warm in his affections, just in his dealings, laborious in his profession, and much addicted to sobriety.

We shall conclude this division of our work, by presenting our readers with the following curious and instructive information in Physiognomy:

Strength of Body is known by a stiff hair, large bones, firm and robust limbs, short muscular neck, firm and erect, the head and breast high, the forehead short, hard, and peaked, with bristly hair, large feet, rather thick than broad, a harsh unequal voice, and choleric complexion.

Weakness of Body is distinguished by a small ill-proportioned head, narrow shoulders, soft skin, and melancholy complexion.

The signs of Long life are strong teeth, a sanguine temperament, middle stature, large, deep, and ruddy lines in the hand, large muscles, stooping shoulders, full chest, firm flesh, clear complexion, slow growth, wide ears, and large eyelids.

Short Life may be inferred from a thick tongue; the appearance of grinders before the age of puberty, thin struggling and uneven teeth confused lines in the hand, of a quick but small growth.

A Good Genius may be expected from a thin skin, middle stature, blue bright eyes, fair complexion, straight pretty strong hair, and affable aspect, the eyebrows joined, moderation in mirth, an open cheerful countenance, and the temples a little concave.

A Dunce may be known by a swollen neck, plump arms, sides, and loins, a round head, concave behind, a large fleshy forehead, pale eyes, a dull heavy look, small joints, snuffing nostrils, and a proneness to laughter, little hands, an ill-proportioned head, either, too big or too little blubber lips, short fingers, and thick legs.

Fortitude is promised from a wide mouth, a sonorous voice, grave, slow, and always equal, upright posture, large eyes, pretty open and steadfast, the hair high above the forehead, the head much compressed or flattened, the forehead square and high, the extremities large and robust, the neck firm though not fleshy, a large corpulent chest, and brown complexion.

Boldness is characterized by a prominent mouth, rugged appearance, rough forehead, arched eyebrows, large nostrils and teeth, short neck, great arms, ample chest, square shoulders, and a froward countenance.

Prudence is generally distinguished by a head which is flat on the sides, a broad square forehead, a little concave in the middle, a soft voice, a large chest, a thin hair, light eyes, either blue, brown or black, large eyes, and an aquiline nose.

A good Memory is commonly attached to those persons who are smaller, yet better formed in the upper than the lower parts, not fat but fleshy, of a fair delicate skin, with the poll of the head uncovered, crooked nose, teeth thick set, large ears with plenty of cartilage.

A *bad Memory* is observable in persons who are larger in their superior than inferior parts, fleshy though dry and bald.—N. B. This is expressly contrary to the opinion of Aristotle, who says; that the superior parts being larger than the inferior signify a good memory, and *vice versa.*

A *good Imagination and thoughtful Disposition* is distinguished by a large prominent forehead, a fixed and attentive look, slow respiration, and an inclination of the head.

A *good Sight* is enjoyed by those persons who have generally black, thick, straight eye-lashes, large bushy eyebrows, concave eyes, contracted as it were inward.

Short-sighted People have a stern, earnest look, small short eyebrows, large pupils and prominent eyes.

Sense of Hearing, those who possess the same in perfection, have ears well furnished with gristle, well channelled and hairy.

The Sense of Smelling is most perfect in those who have large noses, descending very near the mouth, neither too moist nor too dry.

A *nice Faculty of Training* is peculiar to such as have a spongy, porous, soft tongue, well moistened with saliva, yet not too moist.

Delicacy in the Touch belongs to those who have a soft skin, sensible nerves, and nervous sinews, moderately warm and dry.

Irascibility is accompanied by an erect posture, a clear skin, a solemn voice, open nostrils, moist temples, displaying superficial veins, thick neck, equal use of both hands, quick pace, blood-shot eyes, large, unequal, ill-ranged eyes, and choleric disposition.

Timorousness resides where we find a concave neck, pale color, weak-winking eyes, soft hair, smooth plump breast, shrill tremulous voice, small mouth, thin lips, broad thin hands, and small shambling feet.

Melancholy is denoted by a wrinkled countenance, dejected eyes, meeting eyebrows, slow pace, fixed look, and deliberate respiration.

An amorous Disposition may be known by a fair slender face, a redundancy of hair, rough temples, broad forehead, moist shining eyes, wide nostrils, narrow shoulders, hairy hands and arms, well shaped legs.

Gayety attends a serene open forehead, rosy agreeable countenance, a sweet musical tone of voice, an agile body and soft flesh.

Envy appears with a wrinkled forehead, frowning, dejected, and squinting look, a pale melancholy countenance, and a dry rough skin.

Intrepidity often resides in a small body,

with red curled hair, ruddy countenance, frowning eyebrows, arched and meeting, eyes blue and yellowish, large mouth, and red lines in the hand.

Gentleness and Complacency may be distinguished by a soft and moist palm, frequency of shutting the eyes, soft movement, slow speech, soft, straight and lightish-colored hair.

Bashfulness may be discovered by moist eyes, never wide open, eyebrows frequently lowered, blushing checks, moderate pace, slow and submissive speech, bent body, and glowing ears of a purple hue.

Temperance or Sobriety is accompanied with an equal respiration, a moderate-sized mouth, smooth temples, eyes of an ordinary size, either fair or azure, and a short, flat body.

Strength of Mind is signified by light curled hair, a small body, shining eyes, but a little depressed, a grave intense voice, bushy beard, large broad back and shoulders.

Pride stands confessed with arched eyebrows, a large prominent mouth, a broad chest, slow pace, erected head, shrugging shoulders, and staring eyes.

Luxury dwells with a ruddy or pale complexion, downy temples, bald pate, little eyes, thick neck, corpulent body, large nose, thin eyebrows, and hands covered with a kind of down.

Loquacity may be expected from a bushy beard, broad fingers, pointed tongue, eyes of a ruddy hue, a large prominent upper lip, and a sharp pointed nose.

Perverseness may be dreaded, when we perceive a high forehead, firm, short, thick, immoveable neck, quick speech, immoderate laughter, fiery eyes, and short fleshy hands and fingers.

Impudence may be inferred from fiery staring eyes, eager look, circular forehead, round, ruddy countenance, elevated chest, a flat nose, and loud laughter, &c.

As connected with this part of our subject, we subjoin the following Rules.

RULES TO KNOW THE TEMPER AND DISPOSITION OF EVERY ONE.

The signs of a Choleric Disposition, are

1. The habit of the body hot in touch, dry, lean, hard and hairy.
2. The color of the face yellow.
3. A natural dryness of the mouth and tongue.
4. The thirst great and frequent.
5. Activity and inquietude of the body.
6. The pulse hard, swift, and often beating.
7. The spittle bitter.
8. The dreams are most of yellow things, of brawls, of fights, and quarrels.

The Signs of a sanguine Constitution, are

1. The habit of the body hot in touch, fleshy, soft and hairy.
2. The color of the body fresh, sanguine, and lively.
3. A natural and constant blush in the face.
4. The pulse soft, moist, and full.
5. The sweetness of the spittle.
6. Dreams most commonly of red things, of beauty, feasting, dancing, music, and all jovial and pleasing recreations.
7. A continual habit of pleasantness and affability.
8. Often affected with jests, mirth, and laughter.

The Signs of a Phlegmatic Constitution, are

1. The habit of the body cold and moist, in touch soft, fat, gross, and not hairy.
2. A constant natural whiteness, or wanness in the face.
3. The pulse soft, slow, and rare.
4. The thirst little, and seldom desiring drink.
5. The dreams usually are of white things, floods, inundations, and accidents belonging to water.
6. Sleep much and frequent.
7. Slowness and dullness of the body to exercise.

The Signs of a Melancholy Constitution, are

1. The body in touch cold, dry, lean, and smooth.
2. The body of a dark, dull, gloomy, leaden color.
3. The spittle in little quantity, and sour.
4. Pulse little, rare, and hard.
5. The dreams often of black and terrible things—as of spirits, ghosts, dreadful apparitions, choking and beheading; mad beasts, as oxen, wolves, and tigers, ready to devour you.
6. Greatly oppressed with fear.
7. A stability in cogitations, and constancy in the performance of the thing intended.

The Physiognomical Signs of a good Genius, are

A straight erect body, neither over tall or short, between fat and thin, the flesh naturally soft, the skin neither soft nor rough, but a medium between ; the complexion white, verging to a blush of redness ; the hair between hard and soft, usually of a brown color, the head and face of a moderate size, the forehead rather high, the eyes manly, big, and clear, of a blue or hazel color, the aspect mild and humane, the teeth so mixed, that some are broad and some are narrow, a subtle tongue, and the voice be-tween intense and remiss, the neck comely and smooth ; the channel-bone of the throat appearing and moving ; the back and ribs not over fleshy, the shoulders plain and slender, the hands indifferently long and smooth, and equally distant, the nails white, mixed with red, and shining, and the carriage of the body erect in walking.

BOOK THE SIXTH.

CARDIOLOGY ;

Or the Science of Foretelling Events by Cards, Dice and Dominoes.

As many of those events about to happen may be easily gathered from the cards, we have here affixed the definition which each card in the pack bears separately ; by combining them the reader must judge for himself, observing the following directions in laying them out. First, the person whose fortune is to be told, if a *man*, must choose one of the four kings to represent himself—if a *woman*, she must select one of the queens ; then the queen of the chosen king, or the king of the chosen queen will stand for the husband or wife, mistress or lover of the party, whose fortune is to be told, and the knave of the suit for the most intimate person of their family—you must then shuffle and cut the cards well, and let the person whose fortune is to be ascertained, cut them three times, showing the bottom card : this must be repeated three times—then shuffle them again, let them be cut once, and display them in rows on the table, taking care always to have an odd number in each row, nine is the right number, and to place your cards exactly under each other ; after this consult the situation in which the person stands by the definition we have here annexed to each card, and after having repeated it three times, form your conclusions ; remember that every thing is within your circle as far as you can count thirteen any way from the card that represents the person, his wife or her husband, and their intimate friend ; and also that the thirteenth card every way is of the greatest consequence ; either the whole pack, or only the picquet cards may be used.

Another mode with the picquet cards is to shuffle and cut them, take three cards from the top ; if there be two of a suit, take out the highest card ; if three, take all : when you have gone through the pack, shuffle and cut the remainder, and do as before, and repeat the same a third time ; then take a general view of all the cards drawn, and next couple them, a top and a bottom card, then shuffle and cut them into three heaps, laying one apart in the first round to form a fourth heap; the first heap at the left hand relates to yourself entirely, the next to your family; the third is the confirmation of the former two—you must proceed a second and third time, adding each time one to the single card, and then three single cards give the connection of the operation; observe, you must add the card which represents the person whose fortune is consulted to the three, if it be not there already.

We have witnessed a great number of most wonderful and useful conclusions which have been produced by this science and many future events have been foretold; but much depends herein on the ingenuity and skill of the artist, who after having duly obtained the true and full meaning that each card in the pack bears separately, and in its independent state, he must be also most fully enabled to form, judge, and vary all their several mixtures, company, and combinations, which are easily deducted, and calculated by any person of an ordinary common capacity, for these cards (like the planets, men, and other things) are often somewhat altered and changed from their natural state by the mixture of the company in which they are found, which said rule must always be duly attended to throughout the whole course of practice in the same. This divination by cards is a kind of a geomantic lot, and these kind of lots were always held in the highest estimation and repute by the ancients, so that they would perform no work of great importance without first consulting these kind of lots; for whatever divination and predictions of human events are made and formed in this way and manner, must of necessity, besides the lot, have some sublime occult cause, which indeed shall not be a cause by accident, such as Aristotle (and some in our present day) describes fortune to be; for, in the series of causes, a cause by accident can never be the prime and sufficient cause. No, we must look higher, and find out a cause which may know and intend the effect. *It is no matter whether we make cards or any thing else the instrument with which we work in these high mysteries; let the* instrument be what it will, we well know how, and by whom, the particular and general effects of every action, subject, matter, and thing, are always produced; therefore we must not place this in corporeal nature, but in immaterial and corporeal substances, which indeed administer the lot, and dispense the signification of the truth; as in men's souls or departed spirits, or in celestial intelligences. Now that there is in a man's soul a sufficient power and virtue to direct such kind of lots, it is hence manifest, because there is in our souls a divine virtue and similitude, apprehension and power of all things, and all things have a natural obedience to it, and so of necessity have a motion and efficacy to that

which the soul desires, with a strong vehement desire, and all the virtues and operations of natural and artificial things obey it, when it is carried forth into the excess of desire, and then all lots of what kind soever are assisting to the appetite of such a mind, and acquire to themselves wonderful virtues of passages, as from that, so from the celestial opportunity in that hour in which the excess of such like appetite doth most of all exceed in it. *And this is that ground and foundation of all astrological and geomantic questions;* wherefore the mind being thus elevated in the excess of any desire, taketh of itself an hour and opportunity most convenient and efficacious, on which the figure of the heavens being made and set, the artist may then judge the same, and plainly know concerning any subject, matter, or thing, which he may desire or be inquisitive to know. Therefore, whatsoever kind of presage these sort of lots portend and promise, it cannot be made by mere chance, but form a spiritual cause, by virtue whereof the phantasy or hand of him that casteth the lot is moved, either by that power which proceeds from the soul of the operator, through the great excess of his affection, or from a celestial influence, or from a certain spirit assisting or moving from on high. Let the said instruments, which are used in these kind of operations, be made and composed of what they will, whether of Cards, or Geomancy, or any thing else, the effect is still the same, seeing that there are a kind of certain lots that have a divine power of oracles, and are as it were indexes of divine judgment.

This method of using the cards is both innocent and will afford you amusement, while that common, destructive, and most pernicious habit of *gaming*, would otherwise tend to promote and complete the ruin of both your soul and body.

How many very respectable females have there been thus ruined. How many fine young men have there been brought to the scaffold, and other such wretched doleful places, by this most dangerous vice, gaming! We have many times seen and witnessed, even in common families, living in country villages, that the *losers* (even when they have been playing for nothing) have had their countenances deranged and disfigured to an excessive degree, accompanied by language the most diabolical they could possibly invent, in order to vent their rage and passion on what they term ill-luck, even to the utter destruction of their souls and bodies, together with the discomposure and abuse of the company in which they chance to be mixed, and are both a disgrace to themselves and all around them; yet this is what they generally call *an innocent game of cards;* let us ask our readers what must be the case when they are playing for large and considerable sums of money! then their peace of mind, and the happiness and tranquility of their poor unfortunate families must go to ruin.—Reader, let us always avoid such destructive and most dangerous company; lest we, like a great many other such unfortunate beings, may chance to meet our repentance when it comes too late.

The Ace of Clubs,

Is a letter, and promises great wealth, much prosperity in life, and tranquility of mind.

The King of Clubs,

Announces a man who is humane, upright, affectionate, and faithful in all his engagements—he will be happy himself, and make every one with whom he has connection so if he can.

The Queen of Clubs,

Shows a tender, mild, and rather amorous disposition; one that will probably yield her maiden person to a generous lover before the matrimonial knot be tied; but that they will be happy, love each other, and be married.

The Knave of Clubs,

Shows a generous, sincere, and zealous friend, who will exert himself warmly for your interest and welfare.

The Ten of Clubs,

Denotes great riches to come speedily from an unexpected quarter—but it also threatens that you will at the same time lose some very dear friend.

The Nine of Clubs,

Shows that you will displease some of your friends by too steady an adherence to your own way of thinking nor will your success in the undertaking reconcile them to you, or procure you your own approbation.

The Eeight of Clubs,

Shows the person to be covetous, and extremely fond of money; that he will obtain it, but that it will rather prove a torment than a comfort to him, as he will not make a proper use of it.

The Seven of Clubs,

Promises the most brilliant fortune, and the most exquisite bliss that this world can afford; but beware of the opposite sex, from them you can alone experience misfortune.

The Six of Clubs,

Shows you will engage in a very lucrative partnership, and that your children will behave well.

The Five of Clubs,

Declares that you will shortly be married to a person who will mend your circumstances.

The Four of Clubs,

Shows incontinence for the sake of money, and frequent change of object.

The Tray of Clubs,

Shows that you will be three times married, and each time to a wealthy person.—This card will equally answer for a woman's being kept by three rich men according to her station.

The Deuce of Clubs,

Shows that there will be some unfortunate opposition to your favorite inclination, which will disturb you.

The Ace of Diamonds,

Shows a person who is fond of rural sports, a great builder, and a gardener; one who delights in planting, and lays out groves, woods, shrubberies, and other amusements; but that his enterprises of this nature will have success or disappointment according to the cards that are near it—likewise signifies a letter and a ring.

The King of Diamonds,

Shows a man of fiery temper, preserving his anger long, seeking for opportunities of revenge, and obstinate in his resolutions.

The Queen of Diamonds,

Signifies that the woman will be a steady and industrious housekeeper; that she will be fond of company, be a coquette, and not over virtuous.

The Knave of Diamonds,

However nearly related, will look more after his own interest than yours; he will be tenacious of his own opinion, and will not fly off if contradicted.

The Ten of Diamonds,

Signifies a journey—promises a country husband or wife with great wealth and many children; the next card to it will tell the number of children—it also signifies a purse of gold.

The Nine of Diamonds,

Declares that the person will be of a roving disposition; never contented with his lot, and for ever meeting with vexations and disappointments, and risk a shameful end.

The Eight of Diamonds,

Shows that the persons in their youth will be enemies to marriage, and thus run the risk of dying unmarried; but if they marry, it will be with a person whose disposition is so ill-assorted to theirs, that it will be the cause of misfortunes.

The Seven of Diamonds,

Shows that you will spend your happiest days in the country, where, if you remain, your happiness will be uninterrupted; but if you come to town you will be tormented by the infidelity of your partner, and the squandering of your substance.

The Six of Diamonds,

Shows an early marriage, and premature widowhood; but that your second marriage will probably make you worse off.

The Five of Diamonds,

Shows you a well assorted marriage with a mate who will punctually perform the hymeneal duties; and that you will have good children, who will keep you from grief.

The Four of Diamonds,

Shows the incontinence of the person you will be married to, and very great vexation to yourself, through the whole course of your life.

The Tray of Diamonds,

Shows that you will be engaged in quarrels, lawsuits, and domestic disagreements; your partner for life will be of a vixen and abusive temper, fail in the performance of the nuptial duties, and make you unhappy.

The Deuce of Diamonds,

Shows that your heart will be engaged in love at an early period; that your parents will not approve your choice; and that if you marry without their consent, they will hardly forgive you.

The Ace of Hearts,

Signifies merry-making, feasting, and good humor; if the ace be attended by *Spades* it foretells quarrelling in your cups, and ill temper to your family while you are in a state of intoxication; if by *Hearts*, it shows cordiality and affection between the parties; if by *Diamonds*, your feast will be from home, perhaps in the country; if by *Clubs*, the occasion of the meeting will be upon some bargain or agreement; if your ace of hearts is in the neighborhood of face-cards of both sexes, with *Clubs* near, it will be about a match-making, if all the face-cards are kings or knaves, or both, it will concern the buying or selling of some personal property; if all queens, it regards conciliation between parties; and if queens and knaves, it will be about their conciliation and re-union of a married couple.

The King of Hearts,

Shows a man of a fair complexion, of an easy and good-natured disposition, but inclined to be hasty and passionate, and rash in his undertakings.

The Queen of Hearts,

Shows a woman of a very fair complexion, or of great beauty; her temper rather fiery, verging on the termigant; one who will not make an obedient wife, nor one who will be very happy in her own reflections.

The Knave of Hearts,

Is a person of no particular sex, but always the dearest friend or nearest relation of the consulting party, ever active and intruding, equally jealous of doing harm or good as the whim of the moment strikes, passionate and hard to be reconciled, but always zealous and warm in the cause of consulting party, though probably not according to their fancy, as they will be as industrious to prevent their schemes as to forward them, if they do not accord with his own disposition.

You must pay great attention to the cards that stand next to the knave, as from them alone you can judge whether the person it represents will favor your inclinations or not.

The Ten of Hearts,

Shows good nature, and many children—it is a corrective to the bad tidings of the cards that may stand next to it, and if its neighboring cards are of good import, it ascertains and confirms their value.

The Nine of Hearts,

Promises wealth, grandeur, and high esteem; if cards that are unfavorable stand near it, you must look for disappointments and a reverse; if favorable cards follow these last at a small distance, expect to retrieve your losses whether of peace or of goods.

The Eight of Hearts,

Points out a strong inclination to get intoxicated: this, if accompanied with unfavorable cards, will be attended with loss of property, decay of health, and falling off of friends; if by favorable cards, it indicates reformation and recovery from the bad consequences of the former.

The Seven of Hearts,

Shows the person to be of a fickle and unfaithful disposition, addicted to incontinence, and subject to the mean art of recrimination to excuse themselves, although without foundation.

The Six of Hearts,

Shows a generous, open, and credulous disposition, easily imposed upon, and ever the dupe of flatterers, but the good-natured friend of the distressed.—If this card comes before your king or queen you will be the dupe; if after you will have the better.

The Five of Hearts,

Shows a wavering unsteady disposition, never attached to one object, and free from any violent passion or attachment.

The Four of Hearts,

Shows that a person will not be married until very late in life, and that this will probably proceed from a too great delicacy in making a choice.

The Tray of Hearts,

Shows that your own imprudence will greatly contribute to your experiencing the ill-will of others.

The Deuce of Hearts,

Shows that extraordinary success and good fortune will attend the person; though if unfavorable cards attend, this will be a long time delayed.

The Ace of Spades,

Totally relates to the affairs of love, without specifying whether lawful or unlawful.

The King of Spades,

Shows a man who is ambitious, and certainly successful at court or with some great man, who will have it in his power to advance him; but let him beware of a reverse.

The Queen of Spades,

Shows a person that will be corrupted by the great of both sexes—if she is handsome great attempts will be made on her virtue.

The Knave of Spades,

Shows a person who, although they have your welfare at heart, will be too indolent with zeal, unless you take frequent opportunities of arousing their attention.

The Ten of Spades,

Is a card of bad import; it will in a great measure counteract the good effect of the other cards; but unless it be seconded by other unfortunate cards, its influence may be gotten over.

The Nine of Spades,

Is the worst card in the whole pack, it portends dangerous sickness, a total loss of fortune, cruel calamity, and endless dissensions in your family.

The Eight of Spades,

Shows that you will experience strong opposition from your friends, whom you imagine to be such; if this card comes close to you, abandon your enterprise, and adopt another plan.

The Seven of Spades,

Shows the loss of a most valuable friend, whose death will plunge you into very great distress.

The Six of Spades,

Announces a mediocrity of fortune, and very great uncertainty in your undertakings.

The Five of Spades,

Will give very little interruption to your success: it promises you good luck in the choice of a companion for life, that you will meet with one very fond of you, and immoderately attached to the joys of Hymen, but shows your temper to be rather sullen.

The Four of Spades,

Shows speedy sickness, and that your friends will injure your fortune.

The Tray of Spades,

Shows that you will be unfortunate in marriage, that your partner will be incontinent, and that you will be made unhappy. It always signifies tears,

The Deuce of Spades,

Always signifies a coffin, but whom it is for must depend entirely on the other cards that are near it. It foretells grievous affliction, spite, quarrelling, and death.

CURIOUS GAMES WITH CARDS,

By which Fortunes are told in a singular and most diverting manner.

LOVERS' HEARTS.

Four young persons, but not more, may play at this game; or three, by making a dumb hand, or steeping partner, as at whist. Play this game exactly the same in every game, making the queen, whom you call Venus, above ace, the aces in this game only standing for one, and hearts must be first led off by the person next the dealer. He or she who gets most tricks this way (each taking up their own, and no partnership) will have most lovers, and the king and queen of hearts in one hand shows matrimony at hand; but woe to the unlucky one that gets no tricks at the deal, or does not hold a heart in their hand, they will be unfortunate in love, and long tarry before they marry.

CUPID AND HYMEN.

Three are enough for this game, the nines, the threes, and the aces; deal them equally; those who hold kings, hold friends; queens are rivals; knaves, shame; knave alone, lover; three, surprises; ace, sorrow; two together, shows a child before marriage; if a king alone is in her hand with the aces, she stands a good chance; but if a queen is with him, she will never marry the father; the nine of hearts gives the wish that you have most at heart; the nine of diamonds, money; and the nine of clubs, a new gown or coat; but the nine of spades is sorrow. A queen and a knave in one hand, bids fair for a secret intrigue.

HYMEN'S LOTTERY.

Let each one present deposit any sum agreed on, but of course some trifle; put a complete pack of cards, well shuffled, in a bag or reticule. Let the party stand in a circle, and the bag being handed around, each draw three. Pairs of any are favorable omens of some good fortune about to occur to the party, and gets from the pool the sum back that each agreed to pay. The king of hearts is here made the god of love, and claims double, and gives a faithful swain to the fair one who has the good fortune to draw him; if Venus, the queen of hearts is with him, it is the conquering prize, and clears the pool; fives and nines are reckoned crosses and misfor-

tunes, and pay a forfeit of the sum agreed on to the pool, besides the usual stipend at each new game; three nines at one draw shows the lady will be an old maid; three fives, a bad husband.

MATRIMONY.

Let three, five, or seven young women stand in a circle, and draw a card out of a bag; she who gets the highest card out, will be married first of the company, whether she be at the present time maid, wife, or widow; and she who has the lowest, has the longest time to stay ere the sun shines on her wedding-day; she who draws the ace of spades will never bear the name of wife; and she who has the nine of hearts in this trial, will have one lover too many to her sorrow.

CUPID'S PASTIME.

By this game you may amuse yourself and friends, and at the same time learn some curious particulars of your future fate; and though apparently a simple, yet it is a sure method, as several young persons have acknowledged to the sybil who first presented them with the rules.

Several may play at the game, it requiring no number, on leaving out nine on their board, not exposed to view; each person puts a halfpenny in the pool, and the dealer double. The ace of diamonds is made principal, and takes all the other aces, &c. like Pam at Loo; twos and threes in your hand are luck; four, a continuance in your present state; fives, trouble; sixes, profit; sevens, plague; eight, disappointments; nines, surprises; tens, settlement; knaves, sweethearts; kings and queens, friends and acquaintances; ace of spades, death; ace of clubs, a letter; and the ace of diamonds, with the ten of hearts, marriage.

The ace of diamonds being played first, or if it be not cut, the dealer calls for the queen of hearts, which takes next; if the ace be not cut, and the queen conquers, the person who played her will marry that year without a doubt, though it may perhaps seem unluckily at the time; but if she loses her queen, she must wait longer: the ace and queen being called, the rest go in rotation; as at whist, kings taking queens, queens knaves, and so on, and the more tricks you have, the more money you get off the board on the division of each game; those who hold the nine of spades will soon have some trouble, and they are also to pay a penny to the board; but the fortunate fair one who holds the queen and knave of hearts in the same hand, will soon be married; or if she is already within the pale of matrimony, she will have a great rise in life by means of her husband: those who hold the ace of diamonds and queen of hearts, clear the money off the board, and end that game; it also betokens great prosperity

DICE.

This is a certain and innocent way of finding out common occurrences about to take place. Take three dice, shake them well in the box with your left hand, and then cast them out on a board or table, on which you had previously drawn a circle with chalk, but never throw on Monday or Wednesday.

THREE—a pleasing surprise.
FOUR—a disagreeable one.
FIVE—a stranger who will prove a friend.
SIX—loss of property.
SEVEN—undeserved scandal.
EIGHT—merited reproach.
NINE—a wedding.
TEN—a christening, at which some important event will occur to you.
ELEVEN—a death that concerns you.
TWELVE—a letter, speedily.
THIRTEEN—tears and sighs.
FOURTEEN—a new admirer.
FIFTEEN—beware that you are not drawn into some trouble or plot.
SIXTEEN—a pleasant journey.
SEVENTEEN—you will either be on the water, or have dealing with those belonging to it, to your advantage.
EIGHTEEN—a great profit, rise in life, or some most desirable good will happen almost immediately; for the answers to the dice are always fulfilled within nine days. To show the same number twice at one trial, shows news from abroad, be the number what they may. If the dice roll over the circle, the number thrown goes for nothing, but the occurrence shows sharp words, and if they fall to the floor it is blows; in throwing out the dice, if one remains on the top of the other, it is a present, of which I would have the females take care.

DOMINOES.

Lay them with their faces on the table, and shuffle them; then draw one, and see the number.—N. B. Never play on a Friday.
DOUBLE-SIX—receiving a handsome sum of money.
SIX-FIVE—going to a public amusement.
SIX-FOUR—law-suits.
SIX-THREE—ride in a coach.
SIX-TWO—present of clothing.
SIX-ONE—you will soon perform a friendly action.
SIX-BLANK—guard against scandal, or you will suffer by your inattention.
DOUBLE-FIVE—a new abode to your advantage.
FIVE-FOUR—a fortunate speculation.
FIVE-THREE—a visit from a superior.
FIVE-TWO—a water-party.

FIVE-ONE—a love intrigue.
FIVE-BLANK—a funeral, but not of a relation.
DOUBLE-FOUR—drinking liquor at a distance.
FOUR-THREE—a false alarm at your house.
FOUR-TWO—beware of thieves or swindlers.—Ladies, take notice of this; it means more than it says.
FOUR-ONE—trouble from creditors.
FOUR-BLANK—receive a letter from an angry friend.
DOUBLE-THREE—sudden wedding, at which you will be vexed.
THREE-TWO—buy no lottery tickets, not enter into any game of chance, or you will lose.
THREE-ONE—a great discovery at hand.
THREE-BLANK—an illegitimate child.
DOUBLE-TWO—you will be plagued by a jealous partner.
TWO-ONE—you will mortgage or pledge some property very soon.
DOUBLE-ONE—you will soon find something to your advantage in the street or road.
DOUBLE-BLANK—the worst presage in all the set of dominoes; you will soon meet trouble from a quarter for which you are quite unprepared.

It is useless for any person to draw more than three dominoes at one time of trial, or in one and the same month, as they will only deceive themselves; shuffle the dominoes each time of choosing; to draw the same domino twice makes the answer stronger.

BOOK THE SEVENTH.

THE ART OF FORETELLING FUTURE EVENTS

BY CHARMS, SPELLS, AND INCANTATIONS,

To be resorted to at certain seasons of the year, and on particular Fasts and Festivals; by which Dreams, Tokens, and other insights into Futurity may be obtained, but more particularly with regard to marriage.

Magic Laurel.

Rise between three and four in the morning of your birth-day, with cautious secrecy; so as to be observed by no one, and pluck a sprig of laurel; convey it to your chamber, and hold it over some lighted brimstone for five minutes, which you must carefully note by a watch or dial; wrap it in a white linen cloth or napkin, together with your own name written on writing paper, and that of the young man who addresses you (or if there is more than one, write all the names down;) write also the day of the week, the date of the year, and the age of the moon; then haste and bury it in the ground, where you will be sure it will not be disturbed for three days and three nights; then take it up and place the parcel under your pillow for three nights, and your dreams will be truly prophetic as to your destiny.

The Three Keys.

Purchase three small keys, each at a different place, and going to bed tie them together with your garter, and place them in your left hand glove, along with a small flat dough cake, on which you have pricked the first letters of your sweetheart's name; put them in your bosom when you retire to rest; if you are to have that young man you will dream of him, but not else.

This charm is the most effectual on the first or third of a new moon.

The Card Charm.

Select all the hearts and diamonds from the pack, put them in one of your stockings, and place them under your pillow any Friday night: as soon as you wake on Saturday morning, provided the fourth hour has struck, not else, draw a card; according to the number of pips, so many years will elapse before you appear at the altar of Hymen. Hearts show a loving husband, diamonds the richest husband or wife; the kings show that you will never marry; the queen, a troublesome rival; the knave of diamonds, a fatal seduction; and the knave of hearts, early widowhood.

The magic Ring.

Borrow a wedding ring, concealing the purpose for which you borrow it; but no widow's or pretended marriage will do, it spoils the charm; wear it for three hours at least before you retire to rest, and then suspend it by a hair off your head over your pillow; write within a circle resembling a ring, the sentence from the matrimonial service, beginning with, *with this ring I thee wed*, and over the circle write your own name in full length, and the figures that stand for your age; place it under your pillow and your dream will fully explain who you are to marry, and what kind of a fate you will have with them. If your dream is too confused to remember it, or you do not dream at all, it is a certain sign you will never be a bride.

The Witches' Chain.

Let three young women join in making a long chain, about a yard will do, of Christmas, juniper, and misletoe berries, and at the end of every link put an oak acorn. Exactly before midnight let them assemble in a room by themselves, where no one can disturb them; leave a window open, and take the key out of the keyhole and hang it over the chimney-piece; have a good fire, and place in the midst of it a long

thinnish log of wood, well sprinkled with oil, salt, and fresh mould, then wrap the chain round it, each maiden having an equal share in the business; then sit down, and on your left knee let each fair one have a prayer-book opened at the matrimonial service. Just as the last acorn is burnt, the future husband will cross the room; each one will see her own proper spouse, but he will be invisible to the rest of the wakeful virgins. Those that are not to wed will see a coffin, or some misshapen form, cross the room; go to bed instantly, and you will have remarkable dreams. This must be done either on a Wednesday or Friday night, but no other.

The nine Keys.

Get nine small keys, they must all be your own by begging or purchase, (borrowing will not do, nor must you tell what you want them for;) plait a three-plaited band of your own hair, and tie them together, fastening the ends with nine knots; fasten them with one of your garters to your left wrist on going to bed, and bind the other garter round your head, then say—

St. Peter take it not amiss,
To try your favor I've done this;
You are the ruler of the keys,
Favor me then, if you please;
Let me then your influence prove,
And see my dear and wedded love.

This must be done on the eve of St. Peter's and is an old charm used by the maidens of Rome in ancient times who put great faith in it.

The Mysterious Watch.

Request any person to lend you his watch, and ask him if it will go when laid on the table. He will, no doubt, answer in the affirmative; in which case, place it over the end of the concealed magnet, and it will presently stop. Then mark the precise spot where you placed the watch, and moving the point of the magnet, give the watch to another person, and desire him to make the experiment; in which he not succeeding, give it to a third (at the same time replacing the magnet,) and he will immediately perform it, to the great chagrin of the second party.

This experiment cannot be effected, unless you take the precaution to use a very strongly impregnated magnetic bar, and that the balance wheel of the watch be of steel, which may be ascertained by previously opening it, and looking at the works.

The Magic Rose.

Gather your rose on the 27th of June, and, let it be full blown, and as bright a red as you can get; pluck it between the hours of three and four in the morning, take care to have no witness of the transaction; convey it to your chamber, and hold it over a chafing dish, or any convenient utensil, for the purpose, in which there is charcoal and sulphur of brimstone, hold your rose over the smoke about five minutes, and you will see it have a wonderful effect on the flower. Before the rose gets the least cool, put it in a sheet of writing-paper, on which is written your own name and that of the young man you love best; also the date of the year and the name of the morning star that has the ascendancy at that time; fold it up, and seal it neatly with three separate seals, then run and bury the parcel at the foot of the tree from which you gathered the flower; here let it remain untouched till the 6th of July, take it up at midnight, go to bed and place it under your pillow, and you will have a singular and most eventful dream before morning, or at least before your usual time of rising. You may keep the rose under you three nights without spoiling the charm; when you have done with the rose and paper, be sure to burn them.

Midsummer-day Charm, to know your husband's Trade.

Exactly at twelve, on Midsummer-day, place a bowl of water in the sun, pour in some boiling pewter as the clock is striking, saying thus :—

Here I try a potent spell,
Queen of love, and Juno tell,
In kind union unto me,
What my husband is to be,
This the day, and this the hour,
When it seems you have the power,
For to be a maiden's friend,
So, good ladies, condescend.

A tobacco-pipe full is enough. When the pewter is cold, take it out of the water, and drain it dry in a cloth, and you will find the emblems of your future husband's trade quite plain. If more than one you will marry twice; if confused and no emblems, you will never marry; a coach shows a gentleman for you.

St. Agnes' day.—Charm to know who your husband shall be.

Falls on the 21st of January : you must prepare yourself by a twenty-four hours' fast, touching nothing but pure spring water, beginning at midnight on the 20th to the same again on the 21st; then go to bed, and mind you sleep by yourself, and do not mention what you are trying to any one, or it will break the spell; go to rest on your left side, and repeat these lines three times—

St. Agnes be a friend to me,
Is the gift I ask of thee ;
Let me this night my husband see—

and you will dream of your future spouse; if you see more than one in your dream, you will wed two or three times, but if you sleep and dream not, you will never marry.

St. Magdalene.

Let three young women assemble on the eve of this saint in an upper apartment, where they are sure not to be disturbed, and let no one try whose age is more than 21, or it breaks the charm ; get rum, wine, gin, vinegar, and water, and let each have a hand in preparing the potion. Put it in a ground glass vessel, no other will do ; then let each young woman dip a sprig of rosemary in, and fasten it in her bosom, and taking three sips of the mixture, get into bed ; and the three must sleep together, but not a word must be spoken after the ceremony begins, and you will have true dreams, and of such a nature that you cannot possibly mistake your future destiny. It is not particular as to the hour in which you retire to rest.

A Christmas Spell.

Steep misletoe berries, to the number of nine, in a mixture of ale, wine, vinegar, and honey, take them on going to bed, and you will dream of your future lot; a storm in this dream is very bad; it is most likely you will then marry a sailor, who will suffer a shipwreck at sea; but to see either sun, moon, or stars, it is an excellent presage; so are flowers; but a coffin is an index of a disappointment in love.

A Lent Charm.

To be tried on any Friday in Lent, Good Friday excepted, when it is improper to try any thing of the kind, and the mind ought to be more seriously disposed. Write twelve letters of the common alphabet on separate pieces of card, also twelve figures, and the same number of blank cards, then put them in a bag and shake them well, and let each present draw one; a blank shows a single life; a figure, intrigue, or crim con. and a letter a happy marriage.

Valentine.

If you receive one of those love tokens, and cannot guess at the party who sent, or are in any doubt, the following method will explain it to a certainty: prick the fourth finger of your left hand, and with a crow-quill write on the back of the valentine the day and hour in which you were born, and the date of the year, also of the present one, the moon's age, and the name of present morning star, all of which you will find in the almanac, and the sign into which the sun has entered ; try this on the first Friday after you receive the valentine, but do not go to bed till midnight; place the paper in your left shoe, and put it under your pillow; lay on your left side, and repeat three times—

St. Valentine, pray condescend
To be this night a maiden's friend ;
Let me now my lover see,
Be he of high or low degree ;
By a sign his station show,
Be it weal or be it wo,
Let him come to my bed-side,
And my fortune thus decide.

The young woman will be sure to dream of the identical person who sent the valentine, and may guess by the other particulars of the dream, if or not he is to be her spouse.

Fast of St. Anne's.

This is a hard trial, but what is not impossible to any young lady who wishes to know her lot in marriage, that most important change in human life.

Prepare yourself three days previous to the eve of this female saint, by living on bread and water and sprigs of parsley, and touch no other thing whatever, or our labor will be lost ; the eve begins at the sixth hour. Go to bed as soon as you once begin to undress; get into bed, lay on your left side with your head as low as possible, then repeat the following verse three times:—

St. Anne, in silver clouds descend,
Prove thyself a female's friend ;
Be it good, or bring it harm,
Let me have knowledge from the charm
Be it husbands one, two, three
Let me in rotation see ;
And if fate decrees me four
(No modest maid can wish for more.)
Let me view them in my dream,
Fair and clearly to be seen ;
But if the stars decree
Perpetual virginity,
Let me sleep on, and dreaming not,
I shall know my single lot.

Cupid's Nosegay.

On the first night of the new moon in July, take a red rose, a white rose, a yellow flower, a blue one, a sprig of rue and rosemary, and nine blades of long grass ; bind all together with a lock of your own hair ; kill a white pigeon sprinkle the nosegay with the blood from the heart, and some common salt, wrap the flowers in a white handkerchief, and lay it under your head on the pillow, when you go to rest, and before morning you will see your fate as clear as if you had your nativity cast by the first astrologer in the kingdom ; not only in respect to love, lovers, or marriage, but in the other most important affairs of your life ; storms in this dream foretell great trouble, &c.

Love presents and witching Spells.

Take three hairs from your head, roll them up in a small compact form, and anoint them with three drops of blood, from the left hand fourth finger, choosing this because the anatomists say a vein goes from that finger to the heart : wear this in your bosom (taking care that none knows the secret) for nine days and nights : then enclose the hair in a secret cavity of a ring or a brooch, and present it to your lover. While it is in his possession, it will have the effect of preserving his love, and leading his mind to dwell on you. A chain or plait of your own hair mixed with that of a goat, and anointed with nine drops of the essence of ambergris, will have similar effect. Flowers prepared with your own blood, will have an effect on your lover's mind; but the impression will be very transient, and fade with the flowers. If your love should be fortunate and likewise married to the object of your wishes never reveal to him the nature of the present you made him, or it may have the fatal effect of turning love into hate.

The Ring and Olive Branch.

Buy a ring, it matters not it being gold, so as it has the resemblance of a wedding ring, and it is best to begin this charm on the person's birthday. Pay for the ring with some trifling coin, for whatever change is received, must be given to the first beggar you meet in the street ; and if no one asketh alms of you, give it to some poor person; there will be no occasion to go far before one can be found to whom it will be acceptable—be sure to note what might be said in return, such as GOD BLESS YOU, or wishing good fortune, as is usual. When arrived at home, write it down on a sheet of paper, at each of four corners, and in the middle put the two first letters of your name, your age, and the letters of the planets then reigning, as morning and evening stars ; get a branch of olive, and fasten the ring on the stalk with a string or thread, which has been steeped all day in honey and vinegar, or any composition of opposite qualities, very sweet and very sour ; cover your ring and stalk with the written paper carefully wrapped round and round ; wear it in your bosom till the ninth hour of the night, then repair to the next church-yard and bury the charm in the grave of a young man who died unmarried : and, while you are so doing, repeat the letters of your christain name three times backward; return home, and keep as quiet a possible, till you go to bed which must be before eleven o'clock; put a light in your chimney, or some safe place; and, before midnight, or just about that time, your husband that is to be, will present himself at the foot of the bed, but will presently disappear. If you are not to marry, none will come; and, in that case, if you dream before morning, of children, it shows you will have them unmarried; and if you dream of crowds of men, beware of prostitution.

Love Letters.

On receiving a love letter that has any particular declaration in it, lay it wide open; then fold it in nine folds, pin it next to your heart, and thus wear it till bed time; then place it in your left hand glove, and lay it under your head. If you dream of gold, diamonds, or any other costly gem, your lover is true, and means what he says; if of white linen, you will lose him by death; and if of flowers, he will prove false. If you dream of his saluting you, he is at present false, and means not what he professes, but only to draw you into a snare.

To know if a Woman with Child will have a Girl or Boy.

Write the proper names of the father and the mother, and of the month she conceived with child, and likewise adding all the numbers of those letters together, divide them by seven; and then if the remainder be even, it will be a girl if uneven, it will be a boy.

To know if a Child new-born shall live or not.

Write the proper names of the father and mother, and of the day the child was born, and put to each letter its number, as you did before, and unto the total sum, being collected together, put twenty-five, and then divide the whole by seven; and then, if it be even, the child shall die; but if it be uneven, the child shall live.

To know if any one shall enjoy their love or not.

Take the number of the first letter of your name, the number of the planet, and the day of the week; put all these together, and divide them by thirty; if it be above, it will come to your mind, and if below, to the contrary: and mind that number which exceeds not thirty.

To find out the two first letters of a future Wife's or Husband's Name.

Take a small Bible and the key of your front street-door, and having opened to Solomon's

Songs, chap. viii. ver. 6 and 7, place the wards of the key on those two verses, and let the bow of the key be about an inch out of the top of the Bible; then shut the book, and tie it round with your garter, so as the key will not move, and the person who wishes to know his or her future husband or wife's signature, must suspend the Bible, by putting the middle finger of the right hand under the bow of the key, and the other person in like manner on the other side of the bow of the key, who must repeat the following verses, after the other person's saying the alphabet, one letter to each time repeating them. It must be observed, that you mention to the person who repeats the verses, before you begin, which you intend to try first, whether sirname or christian name; and take care to hold the Bible steady and when you arrive at the appointed letter the book will turn round under your finger, and that you will find to be the first letter of your intended's name.

Solomon's Songs, chap. viii. ver. 6 and 7.

"Set me as a seal upon thine heart, as a seal upon thine arm; for love is strong as death, jealousy is cruel as the grave; the coals thereof are coals of fire, which hath a most vehement flame.

"Many waters cannot quench love, neither can the floods drown it; if a man would give all the substance of his house for love, it would be utterly contemned."

To know how soon a Person will be Married.

Get a green pea-pod, in which are exactly nine peas, hang it over the door, and then take notice of the next person who comes in, who is not of the family, and if it proves a bachelor, you will certainly be married within that year.

On any Friday throughout the year—Take rosemary flowers, bay leaves, thyme, and sweet marjoram, of each a handful; dry these, and make them into a fine powder then take a teaspoonful of each sort, mix the powders together; then take twice the quantity of barley flour and make the whole into cake with the milk of a red cow. This cake is not to be baked, but wrapped in clean writing-paper, and laid under your head any Friday night. If the person dreams of music, she will wed those she desires, and that shortly; if of fire, she will be crossed in love; if a church, she will die single. If any thing is written, or the least spot of ink is on the paper, it will not do.

To know what Fortune your future Husband will be.

Take a walnut, a hazel-nut, and nutmeg; grate them together, and mix them with butter and sugar, and make them up into small pills, of which exactly nine must be taken on going to bed; and according to her dreams, so will be the state of the person she will marry. If a gentleman, of riches; if a clergyman, of white linen; if a lawyer, of darkness; if a tradesman, of odd noises and tumults; if a soldier or sailor, of thunder and lightning; if a servant, of rain.

Bride Cake.

A slice of the bride-cake thrice drawn through the wedding-ring, and laid under the head of an unmarried woman, will make her dream of her future husband.—The same is practiced in the north with a piece of the groaning cheese.

Another way to see a future spouse in a dream: the party inquiring must lie in a different county from that in which she commonly resides, and on going to bed, must knit the left garter about the right-legged stocking, letting the other garter and stocking alone; and as you rehearse the following verse, at every comma knit a knot:

This knot I knit, to know the thing I know not yet,
That I may see, the man that shall my husband be,
How he goes, and what he wears,
And what he does all days and years.

Accordingly in a dream he will appear, with the insignia of his trade or profession.

Another, performed by charming the moon, thus:—at the first appearance of the new moon, immediately after new-year's day, go out in the evening, and stand over the spears of a gate or stile, and looking on the moon, repeat the following lines:—

All hail to thee, moon! all hail to thee!
I pr' thee, good moon, reveal to me
This night, who my husband must be!

The party will then dream of her future husband.

A spell, to be used at any convenient time.

Make a nosegay of various colored flowers, one of a rose, a sprig of rue and some yarrow off a grave, and bind all together with the hair of your head; sprinkle them with a few drops of the oil of amber, using your left hand, and bind the flowers round your head when you retire to rest under your night cap; and put on clean sheets and linen, and your future fate will appear in your dream.

Promise of Marriage.

If you receive a written one, or any declaration to that effect in a letter, prick the words with a sharp-pointed needle on a sheet of paper

quite clear from any writing; fold it in nine folds, and place it under your head when you retire to rest. If you dream of diamonds, castles, or even a clear sky, there is no deceit, and you will prosper; trees in blossom, or flowers, show children: washing or graves, shows you will lose them by death; and water shows they are faithful, but that you will go through severe poverty, with the party for some time, though all may end well.

Strange Bed.

Lay under your pillow a prayer-book, opened at the matrimorial service, bound round with the garters you wore that day, and a sprig of myrtle on the page that says WITH THIS RING I THEE WED, and your dream will be ominous, and you will have your fortune as well told as if you had paid a crown to an astrologer

Acorns.

This is to be tried on the third day of the month between September and March. Let any number of young women, not exceeding nine, and minding that there is an odd one in the company assembled together and each string nine acorns on a separate string, or as many acorns as there are females in company, but not more; wrap them round a long stick of wood, and place it in the fire, just as the clock strikes twelve at night; say not a word, but sit round the fire till all the acorns are consumed, then rake out the ashes, and retire to bed almost directly, repeating—

May love and marriage be the theme,
To visit me in this night's dream;
Gentle Venus, be my friend,
The image of my lover send;
Let me see his form and face,
And his occupation trace;
By a symbol or a sign,
Cupid, forward my design.

Yarrow.

This is a weed commonly found in abundance on graves, toward the close of the spring and beginning of summer. It must be plucked exactly on the first hour of morn, place three sprigs either in your shoe or glove saying—
Good morning, good morning, good yarrow,
And thrice a good morning to thee;
Tell me before this time to-morrow,
Who my true love is to be.

Observe, a young man must pluck the weed off a young maiden's grave, and a female must select that of a bachelor's; retire home to bed without speaking another word, or it dissolves the spell; put the yarrow under your pillow, and it will procure a sure dream on which you may depend.

A Charm, to be used on the eve of any fast directed in the Calendar.

This takes a week's preparation, for you must abstain from meat or strong drink; go not to bed till the clock has struck the midnight hour, and rise before seven the next morning; the whole seven days you must neither play at cards, or any game of chance, nor enter a place of public diversion; when you go to bed on the night of trial eat something very salt, and do not drink after it and you may depend on having very singular dreams, and being very thirsty you will probably dream of liquids; wine is excellent, and shows wealth or promotion: brandy, foreign land; rum, that you will wed a sailor, or one that gets his living on the sea: gin, but a middling life; cordials, variety of fortune; and water, if you drink it, poverty; but to see a clear stream is good.—Children are not good to behold in this dream, nor cards, nor dice, they forebode the loss of reputation, or that you will never marry.

How to make the Dumb-Cake.

In order to make the dumb-cake with perfection, it is necessary strictly to observe the following instructions:—

Let any number of young women take a handful of wheaten flour, (and from the moment the hand touches the flour, not a word is to be spoken by any of them during the process,) and place it on a sheet of white paper; then sprinkle it over with as much salt as can be held betwixt the finger and thumb; then one of the damsels must bestow as much of her own water as will make it into dough; which being done, each of the company must roll it up, and spread it thin and broad; and each person must, at some distance from each other, make the first letters of her Christian and surname, with a large new pin, toward the end of the cake (if more Christian names than one, the first letter of each must be made;) the cake must be then set before the fire, and each person must sit down in a chair, as far distant from the fire as the room will admit, not speaking a single word all this while.

This must be done soon after eleven at night, and between that and twelve each person must turn the cake once, and in a few minutes after twelve, the husband of her who is to be first married will appear to lay his hand on that part of the cake which is marked with her name.

BOOK THE EIGHTH.

ONEIROLOGY;

Or, the Science of Foretelling future Events by Dreams.

ABUSE.—To dream that you are abused and insulted, is a certain sign some dispute will happen between you and some person with whom you have business, therefore, after such a dream, you should be particularly careful of yourself, and be as gentle and mild as possible, that you may not give those with whom you have dealings any advantage over you—if you are in love, be assured that some one has attempted to injure you with the object of your affections, and that they have in a great measure succeeded—you should, therefore, after such a dream, be particularly complaisant and attentive; by this means you will eradicate the unfavorable impressions that have been made against you—if you have a law-suit, keep a sharp lookout after your attorney, for such a dream in that case denotes, that he is endeavoring to sell your cause—avoid, after such a dream, taking a journey by land, or a voyage by sea, for eight and forty hours, because such a dream forebodes accidents by traveling.

ADULTERY.—To dream of the commission of this sin, forebodes great troubles and misfortunes—if you are in love, you will certainly fail in marrying the object of your wishes—if you have a law-suit, it will certainly go against you, by the treachery of those who pretended to be your friends—if you are in business, some heavy loss will happen to you. Such a dream announces, that you are in great danger of losing your liberty—and if you are about to take a voyage by sea, omit it for the present, for you will never reach the destined port. To dream that you were tempted to commit this crime, and that you resisted it, is a happy omen—everything will flourish with you—be sure it is a good time to begin trade after such a dream—if you have a law-suit, all will go in your favor, with credit to yourself, and confusion to your opponents—if you are about to undertake a long journey, it will be pleasant and successful to your object—if you are going to sea, you will have an agreeable voyage, fine weather, and a quick arrival at the port of destination—if you are in love, press the object of your wishes, for they will be gratified.

ABEL. To dream of this second son of Adam, the victim of his brother's vengeance and jealousy, and the first man that stained the earth with his blood, is a favorable omen, portends future elevation and grandeur—if you have a law-suit, it will terminate in your favor—if you are in love, the mistress of your heart will be kind and faithful—if you are about to commence trade, your business will thrive, and you will become rich—if you are a farmer, be sure of good crops the ensuing season—if you are about to undertake a journey, it will be prosperous to you; in short, expect to rise to honors, dignity, and affluence, observe one thing, that should he speak to you in your dream, you should be very careful to mind what he says, as otherwise you may mar all your good fortune, and reverse every benefit that fortune has in store for you.

ABRAHAM. To dream of this Patriarch is favorable to the person who dreams—it in general denotes accumulation of riches and of honor—in a woman, it denotes that she will have many children—if you are in love, it denotes you will have many rivals—if you have a law-suit, it forebodes that many difficulties will occur—if you are in business, then it portends a great increase of your business, and that you will employ many hands to conduct it; you must also be very observant of what he says to you, for he will perhaps inform you how to avoid some misfortune, or how to attain to riches and honors.

ADAM. To dream you see this father of men, this inhabitant of Paradise, who was betrayed by Eve into sin, is a happy omen—if he looks pleasant, be sure you will succeed in whatever you undertake—if you are in love, expect your mistress to smile on your love, and to reward your constancy—if you have a law-suit, expect it to be given much in your favor by the judge—if you are a farmer, expect an abundant crop, and that your pigs, poultry, and cattle, will increase very fast, and be of a good kind, and fetch the best price at market —if you are about to quit your native place, abandon the idea for depend some benefit is in store for you in the place where you had birth—if you have already quitted it, I would advise you, if you can, to return, for there lies your fortune and prosperity: do not undertake journeys, unless, absolutely necessary, for although they would be successful, yet you will be still more fortunate by resting at home; if he looks displeased and angry, then you must use great caution in all your dealings, for some mischief is intended you, but you will get the better of it; but on no account undertake a voyage by sea, neither borrow or lend money, for at least a month or two, because, if you do, you will lose what you lend, and what you borrow will bring you into trouble; be careful if he speaks to you, to mind what he says and observe it as faithfully as you possibly can.

ADVERSARY. To dream you meet with an adversary, denotes that you will overcome some obstacle to your happiness—if you are a lover, you will conquer some powerful rival, and be happy in your love; it also denotes, that your affairs are going on well—if you are soliciting a place, it portends you are about to get it—if you are in trade, it forebodes some good orders, and an increase of business—if you quarrel, and he overcomes you, it is a good sign, for you will conquer all obstacles to your promotion, happiness, and fortune; but, if you conquer him, then it de-

notes that you will never rise to any great preferment by the means you are at present adopting; that many things will miscarry with you, but in general you will be fortunate— should he draw blood of you, you will surely lose your liberty for a time, but will afterward be flourishing and happy.

ACQUAINTANCE. To dream you quarrel or fight with an acquaintance, is an unlucky omen ; it forebodes a division amongst your own family, much to the injury and prejudice of the dreamer —if you are in love, your mistress will prove unfaithful, and marry some other man that she has told you she most hates—if you are in business, some heavy loss will befall you ; you will disagree with some of your best friends on the most trivial matters which will end in an open rupture—if you are a farmer, expect a bad crop, the murtra amongst your cattle ; that your pigs and poultry will fail, and not fetch good prices—if you have a law-suit, depend, that your attorney will neglect you, that your witnesses will be tardy and backward, and that finally you will lose your cause. Do not for some time undertake a journey by land, or a voyage by sea : enter for the present into no new undertaking, for you will be unsuccessful; quit, if you can, your present place of residence ; and, above all, avoid lending money, for you will surely lose it, together with the friendship of those to whom you lend it.

AGUE. To dream you have an ague, denotes nothing very particular, more than that you are in danger of becoming a drunkard, and a glutton. If you have any relation or friend that is ill, it denotes they will recover—and if you have a lawsuit, that it will be settled in your favor—if you are in love, it forewarns you, that if you do not immediately marry, you will lose your mistress—if you dream another has an ague, then it denotes a variety of fortune, that you will sometimes be rich, and sometimes poor ; that you will have much trouble, lose your liberty ; and die before you are fifty. To dream your sweetheart has an ague, is a lucky omen ; it shows you are beloved, and that you will be happy with the object of your wishes, but never very rich.

ANGELS. To dream you see angels in your sleep, is a sure sign, that some one is near you —therefore be mindful of the rest of your dream, for it will come to pass pretty accurately ; should you only dream you see nothing but an angel, or angels, then it denotes health, prosperity, and much happiness, with many children, who will all turn out good. If a woman with child dreams of them, she will have a good time, and perhaps twins—if you are in love, nothing can be more favorable, and all your undertakings will prosper, and be advantageous to you.

APPARITIONS. To dream you see a ghost,

hobgoblin, spectre, and such kind of things, is of a very unfortunate nature, they denote vexation and disappointment—if you are in love, it is a certain sign of your not being beloyed in return, that the object of your affections either hates you or despises you—depend upon it some one is about to deceive you and that you are in the habit of friendship with one who is your most inveterate enemy—do not undertake a journey just at this time, for it will be unfortunate to you—and be careful of contracting debts, for such a dream forebodes great trouble through some one to whom you shall owe money.

ASPS. To dream of asps, denotes that you will become extremely rich, and have great quantities of money by you—if you are in love, it imports that your love will be returned, and that your sweetheart will become through your means extremely wealthy.

BAILIFFS. To dream you are arrested by bailiffs, is a sign you will escape some heavy misfortune; but it also foretells, that your present sweetheart will never marry you, and that you will be over-reached in a bargain.

BACON. To dream of bacon, denotes the death of some friend or relation, and enemies will endeavor to do you a mischief—in love, it denotes disappointment and discontent.

BAGPIPES. To dream of this instrument of Scottish music, indicates, that the dreamer will experience great trouble, and that he will labor to little purpose—in love, it denotes that the marriage state will be full of cares, and that you will in it experience much poverty and distress—It also denotes bad success at sea, and forebodes ship-wreck, and a narrow escape from death.

BASIN. To dream you are eating or drinking out of a basin, is a certain sign that you will soon be in love—but without great care you will not marry the first object of your affections—it denotes prosperity in trade; and to the farmer, a good crop—if you are a seafaring man, it indicates that at the next port you touch you will fall in love.

BATHING. To dream of a bath is a very unpropitious omen; expect after it to experience many hardships and much sorrow—if you are in love, your sweetheart will experience many crosses and losses. But to dream you are bathing yourself in clear water, denotes happiness, prosperity, and success in love—if the water is dirty, then it fortells shame and sorrow, and a disappointment in love.

BEANS. To dream of beans, is an unfavorable dream; it is the forerunner of troubles and quarrels—if you are in love, expect a difference to happen between you and your sweetheart.

BEES. To dream of these little industrious insects, who collect the sweets of every flower, have a variety of interpretations according to their different situations. To dream they sting you, denotes loss of good character, and, if you are in love, of your sweetheart.

To dream you see them at work, is a very lucky dream, it forebodes success by your industry—if you are a farmer be sure of good crops—if you are in love, be sure you will marry the object of your affections, and that you will have many children and become rich. To dream you see them making their honey under your own roof, is the best omen in the world; be sure that it denotes dignity in the state, riches, a good husband or wife, and many good children; in short, that whatever you take in hand will be prosperous—if you are soliciting a place, depend you will gain it, and afterward be promoted. For the rich to dream of bees is rather unlucky; but, to the poor, they denote comfort, affluence, and success.

BEHEADING. To dream you see any one beheaded, is a good omen—if you are in love, you will marry the object of your affections—if you are in a prison, you will speedily gain your liberty—if you are in trouble of any kind, it will speedily vanish—it denotes also that you will see some friend who has long been absent, and that he will be in good health.

BELLS. To dream you hear the bells ringing; denotes a speedy marriage, and that you will receive some very good news.

BUILDINGS. To dream of being amongst buildings, denotes that you will change your present place of residence and that you will make many new friends in life; if you are in love, it foretells your sweetheart is about to remove at a distance from you, and that you will be in danger of losing the affections of your lover by new faces.

BATTLE. To dream you see a battle in the streets forewarns you against secret enemies, who will endeavor to harm you—if you are in love, your sweetheart is false to you.

CAGE. To dream of letting birds out of a cage, denotes a speedy marriage: to a person in business it denotes success, and to a farmer it denotes good crops.

CATS. To dream of these domestic animals, is indicative of much trouble and vexation—it denotes to the lover, that your sweetheart is treacherous—if you keep servants, they are unfaithful, and will rob you. To dream you kill a cat, denotes that you will discover a thief, and prosecute him to conviction—expect also to lose your own liberty through the insincerity of some pretended friend.

CATTLE. To dream you see cattle feeding, denotes great prosperity, and unexpected success; to a lover, it foretells a happy marriage, with many children, and to the man it shows, that his wife will receive some unexpected legacy. To dream you are driving cattle, denotes that you will become rich by industry; if you are in love, it shows that you will have many rivals, but that you will distance them all. To dream you see fat cattle, also denotes a plentiful year. To dream you see lean and hungry cattle, denotes scarcity and famine.

CHICKENS. To dream of a hen and chickens, is the forerunner of ill luck, your sweetheart will betray you and marry another—if you are a farmer, you will have a bad crop, and lose many of your poultry—if you are in trade, some sharper will defraud you—if you go to sea, you will lose your goods and narrowly escape shipwreck.

CLIMBING. To dream you are climbing up a tree, denotes that you will arrive at some honor in the state, and that you will be successful in life—If you are in love, you will marry your sweetheart, after a long courtship. To dream you are climbing up a very steep hill or place, foretells many difficulties in life, and much sickness; if you reach the top, you will get over all your difficulties, and recover from your illness; but if you awake before you have attained the top, you will be disappointed in love, and other projects in life, and die in your next illness.

CHURCH. To dream of a church, is portentous of evil. If you are in a church during divine service, you will be engaged in a lawsuit, or some quarrel, that will go very near to ruin you—if you are in love, your sweetheart is unfaithful, and prefers another—if you expect a place; it forebodes disappointment—if you are in trade, you will never thrive in your present situation.

CROWNS. To dream you see these emblems of royalty, portends success and elevation to dignities either in the church or state; for a maid to dream of a crown, shows she will marry a very industrious man, or one who is rich; her husband will be prosperous in life, and have many children by her; all of whom will do well except the youngest; if you are in trade, you will thrive exceedingly, marry an industrious woman, and become rich. To dream of crown-pieces of money forbodes misfortunes; disappointments in love; prisons, and bad success in trade.

COAL-PIT. To dream you are in a coal-pit, foretells that you will shortly lead a widow to the hymeneal altar—to a maid it denotes a speedy marriage with her sweetheart, who will become rich and rise to honors in the state—to the trader, it indicates that he will shortly be tricked out of a quantity of goods.

COMET. To dream you see one of these extraordinary æthereal substances, is ominous of war, plague, famine, and death—to the lover it forebodes an entire frustration of his hopes—to the farmer, failure of crops, and to the seaman, storms and shipwrecks—after such a dream—change, if possible, you present place of residence.

CUCUMBERS. To dream of cucumbers, denotes recovery to the sick, that you will speedily fall in love, or that if you are in love, you will marry the present object of your affection—it also denotes moderate success in trade—to the sailor they foretell a pleasant voyage, and a sweetheart in a distant clime.

DANCING. To dream you are dancing at a ball, wake, or entertainment, foretells that you will shortly receive some joyful news from a long absent friend, and that you are about to inherit some unexpected legacy—it foretells success and happiness in love—that your sweetheart is kind and true, and will make you very happy in marriage—to the sailor, it denotes a pleasant and successful voyage—increase of children to married persons, and of business to those in trade.

DARKNESS. To dream you are in a very dark place, or that you are in the dark, is a very unfavorable omen—to the lover it denotes the loss of your sweetheart—to the trader, loss by debts, business, and a prison—to the farmer, bad crops—to the sailor, shipwreck and misfortune. To dream you get out of darkness into light, denotes good to the dreamer—if you are in prison, you will speedily be released; if you are accused of a crime, you will be acquitted with honor—if you are in poverty, it foretells you will rise to riches and honor—if you are in love, it denotes a happy marriage, and many children, with an industrious husband or wife—expect also to hear some glad tiding from a far distant country.

DEATH. To dream you see this grim looking bundle of bones, denotes happiness and long life—that you will be either speedily married yourself, or else assist at a wedding. To dream that you are dead, also denotes a speedy marriage, and that you will be successful in all your undertakings—to those that are married it foretells young children, and that they will be dutiful, and give you great comfort. To dream you see another person dead, denotes ill usage from friends—if you are in love, your sweetheart will prove false—if you are in trade, sharpers will take you in—if you are a farmer, you will lose money by horses, and be waylaid as you return from market.

DEER. To dream you see deer in a park, denotes war and famine—to the lover, it foretells some very unpleasant dispute with your sweetheart—to the tradesman it denotes trouble, and a prison through a quarrel with your creditors—to the seaman, it denotes bad success and a stormy voyage—expect after such a dream to quarrel with your friends, and be much injured by it.

DICE. To dream you are playing at dice or backgammon, denotes much good to the dreamer—expect to marry the present object of your affections, to be very happy, and become rich—

it foretells a good legacy—to the farmer, it indicates a very good crop, especially of hay: if you are in trade, you will succeed and arrive at riches and honor.

DIRT. To dream of being in the dirt or mire, or that you are in a bog, or that you are traveling near a very dirty road, or that your clothes and flesh are very dirty, is a very unfavorable omen—it portends sickness, and misfortune—if you have a good place, expect to lose it—if you are in love, expect your sweetheart to discard you—if you are in trade, expect heavy losses, and to be quite reduced—if you are going to sea, it certainly forewarns you of shipwreck, and a loss of goods—it also denotes that the rent of your house or land will be raised upon you.

DITCHES. To dream of deep ditches, steep mountains, rocks, and other eminences, surely foretells danger and misfortune—expect thieves to rob your dwelling—that your children will be undutiful, and bring you into trouble—if you are in love, it foretells unhappiness if you marry your present sweetheart—if you are in trade, it denotes loss of goods, if not of liberty.

DOLPHINS. To dream you see dolphins playing in the water, denotes the loss of your sweetheart and the death of some near relation or friend—it is an unfavorable dream, signifies that your present pursuits will not be for your advantage, the dreamer would do well to quit his present habitation.

DROWNING. To dream you are drowning, or that you see another drowned or drowning, portends good to the dreamer, and denotes that he will escape many difficulties, settle near his native place, marry, have children, and become happy and rich—to the lover, it denotes that your sweetheart is good tempered, and inclined to marry you; if you are a sailor, it foretells a favorable and pleasant voyage.

DRUNKENNESS. To dream you are drunk, is one of those dreams by which the dreamer is forewarned of that of which at present he knows nothing—it denotes, that person whom yet you do not know will become a very good friend, and promote your welfare; that through his means you will acquire riches and honors—to a woman it denotes that she will be beloved by a man who yet she has not seen, who will, if she marries him, make her very happy; and to a man, it denotes that he is tenderly beloved by a woman whom he does not at present think of, who will make him extremely happy, and bring him money.

EARTHQUAKE. To dream of an earthquake, warns you that your affairs are about to take a very great change; if you see many houses tumbled into ruins, then it will be much for the better; should the houses appear to stand, then for the worse—it always denotes changes in the

government, in which the dreamer is much interested; for the lover, it foretells that your sweetheart is about to take a journey, and that it is a great chance if you ever see each other again.

EATING. To dream you are eating, is a very unfavorable omen, it portends disunion amongst your family; losses in trade, and disappointment in love—storms and shipwreck by sea. To dream you see others eating, is of a contrary tendency, and foretells success in all your present enterprises; that your sweetheart is kind and faithful, and that if you marry the present object of your affections that you will grow rich, be happy, and have dutiful children.

ECLIPSE OF THE SUN. To dream you see an eclipse of the sun, denotes that you will lose some male friend, your father, if he be alive; and that you will experience some uneasiness by the means of some treacherous friend: to a woman with child it foretells a son, who will be a great man.

ECLIPSE OF THE MOON. To dream you see an eclipse of the moon, denotes that you will lose some female friend, your mother, if she be living; you will experience great uneasiness on account of a woman; your sweetheart will be unfaithful; poverty will overtake you, and misery end your days.

ELEPHANTS. To dream of an elephant is a very fortunate dream; it denotes an acquirement of riches; if you are in love, it denotes a speedy marriage with your sweetheart, and many children, chiefly boys, who will distinguish themselves by their learning.

FALL. To dream you fall from any very high place, or from a tree, denotes loss of place and goods; if you are in love, it surely indicates that you will never marry the present object of your affections: to the tradesman, it denotes a decline of business: and to the sailor, storms and shipwreck.

FAIR. To dream you are at a fair, is a bad omen; it denotes that some pretended friend is about to do you an injury: if you are in trade, keep a keen look out, for some swindler will certainly attempt to defraud you: if you are a farmer, be careful next time you go to market, for some one will waylay you, attempt to rob you: if you are in love, it denotes that some rival is attempting to rob you of those upon whom you have placed your affections.

FEASTING. To dream you are at a feast, denotes that you will meet with many disappointments, particularly in the thing which you are most anxious about: in love, it forebodes much uneasiness between sweethearts: and to them which are married, it foretells undutiful children, with many heavy losses.

FIELDS. To dream you are in green fields is a very favorable omen: in love, it denotes success and happiness: to the tradesman, success and riches: to the sailor, a pleasant and profitable voyage: to the farmer, plenty and health: if you are soliciting any place of favor be sure you will obtain it. To dream you are in ploughed fields, forebodes some severe disputes that will be brought upon you by some person who has no children: to the lover it denotes disappointment: to the married unhappiness, and undutiful children: to the tradesman, loss of business and a prison. To dream you are in a meadow covered with flowers, is a very favorable omen: to a man it indicates a very handsome wife, who will bring him lovely children, and make him very happy: to a woman, it denotes that she will marry a handsome young fellow, by whom she will have beautiful children, that she will become rich, and live to a good old age; to the tradesman, it betokens success, good orders, and riches: if you are soliciting a place of favor, it portends you will surely obtain it.

FIGHTING. To dream you are fighting, denotes to the lover, that you will lose the object of your affections through a foolish quarrel: it also forebodes much opposition to your wishes, with loss of character and property. After such a dream, I would advise the dreamer to quit his present situation; because such a dream indicates that you will not prosper in it: to the sailor it denotes storms and shipwreck, with disappointment in love.

FIRE. To dream of this subtle element, denotes health and happiness to the lover, marriage with the object of your affections, and many children: it also denotes that you will be very angry with some one on a trifling occasion. To dream you see burning lights descending, as it were from heaven, is a very bad sign indeed: it portends some dreadful accident to the dreamer, such as being hanged, losing your head, having your brains dashed out, breaking your legs, getting into prison, or other strange accidents: to the lover, it also denotes the loss of the affections of your sweetheart: to the tradesman, bad success in business. To dream that you are burnt by fire, denotes great danger, and that enemies will injure you: to the sailor, storms and shipwreck.

FISHING. To dream you are fishing, is a sure sign of sorrow and trouble; if you catch any fish you will be successful in love and business; if you catch none you will never marry your present sweetheart, nor succeed in your present undertakings, if they slip out of your hands after you have caught them, the person you marry will be of a roving disposition, and some pretended friend will deceive you.

FLOODS. To dream of a flood, shows that you will meet with great opposition from rich neighbors, and that a rich rival will attempt to alienate the affections of your mistress: to the tradesman, it denotes law-suits, loss of business,

and a prison: to the sailor it denotes much success by sea, but danger on shore: to the farmer, it indicates loss of cattle, and a dispute with his landlord. To dream you are drowned in a flood, denotes that you will quit your native land, and after many hardships and perils, return to it rich and happy, that you will marry a pretty woman, and have fine children.

FLYING. To dream you are flying, is a very excellent omen: it foretells elevation of fortune; that you will arrive at dignity in the state, and be happy. If you are in love, your sweetheart will be true to you, and if you marry, you will have many children, who will all do well, and be very happy; it indicates that you will take a long journey, which will turn out advantageously to you.

FLOWERS. To dream you are gathering flowers, is a very favorable omen; expect to thrive in every thing you undertake, and that you will be successful in love, marry happily, and have beautiful children; should they wither under your hands, then expect heavy losses in trade; that your sweetheart will die; or if you are married, that you will lose your husband or wife, and also your favorite child.

FORTUNE. To dream you make a sudden fortune, is a very bad omen: to the tradesman, it forebodes losses in trade, quarreling with his creditors, and the loss of liberty: to the lover, it denotes that your sweetheart does not return your love: to the sailor, it indicates storms and shipwrecks. If you are soliciting a place, you will not be successful. To dream you are adopting the means of acquiring a fortune, is favorable, it portends a good legacy and success in love.

FOUNTAIN. To dream you are at a fountain, is a very favorable omen; if the waters are clear, it denotes riches and honors; and in love, it foretells great happiness in the marriage state, and that your sweetheart is of an amiable disposition, and true to you: but if the waters appear muddy, then it denotes vexation and trouble; disappointment in business, inconstancy in your sweetheart, and misery in the marriage state.

FRIEND. To dream you see a friend dead, betokens hasty news of a joyous nature; if you are in love, it foretells a speedy marriage with the object of your affections.

GALLOWS. To dream of the gallows, is a most fortunate omen, it shows that the dreamer will become rich, and arrive at great honors: to the lover, it shows the consummation of his most sanguine wishes: and that by marriage you will become rich and happy, have many children, particularly a son, who will become a great man and be the founder of his family's honor.

GARDEN. To dream you are walking in a garden, is of a very favorable nature; it portends elevation in fortune and dignity : to the lover it denotes great success and an advantageous marriage : to the tradesman, it promises increase of business : to the farmer, plentiful crops: and to the sailor, pleasant and prosperous voyages.

GIFTS. To dream you have any thing given you, is a sign that some good is about to happen to you : it also denotes that a speedy marriage will take place betwixt you and your sweetheart. To dream you have given any thing away, is the forerunner of adversity; and in love, denotes sickness and inconstancy in your sweetheart or partner.

HORSES. To dream of these useful animals is symptomatic of good ; if you are mounted on a fine bony horse, you will marry a rich person, who will do well, and make you happy ; it also shows that you will change your situation in life ; if you fall from your horse difficulties will occur, and some unexpected disaster befall you.

HUNTING. To dream you are hunting a fox, and that he is killed shows much trouble through the pretensions of false friends, but that you will discover them, and overcome all their machinations : if you are hunting a hare, it is indicative of bad success, you will be disappointed in your favorite object, be what it may : hunting a stag, if he is caught alive, denotes good to the dreamer, and that he will be successful in all his present undertakings.

INN. To dream of being in an inn, is a very unfavorable dream, it denotes poverty and want of success in undertakings : expect soon to be yourself, or some of your family, committed to prison : if you are sick, it denotes you will never recover : to the tradesman it shows loss of trade and servants.

KNIVES. To dream of knives, is a very unpropitious omen ; it betokens law-suits, poverty, disgrace, strife, and a general failure in the pursuit of your projects : in love, it shows that your sweetheart is of a bad temper, and unfaithful, and that if you marry, you will live in enmity and misery.

LADDER. To dream that you climb a ladder, is a very good prognostic; it denotes that you will better your situation in life, and arrive at honors in the state : in love, it denotes a happy marriage with the object of your affections, and that you will become by industry rich, and settle your children happily.

LEAPING. To dream you are leaping over walls, bars or gates, is a sign that you will encounter many difficulties in your present pursuits, and that your sweetheart will not marry you : if you are leaping over ditches, drains or hedges, it is a favorable omen, you will be successful in love, trade, or other concerns : it also denotes that you will enter into a partnership with more than one person, by which you will accumulate riches, and become very respectable.

LION. To dream of seeing this king of beasts, denotes that you will appear before your betters, and that you will be promoted to some lucrative office, accumulate riches, and marry a woman of great spirit : it argues success in trade, and prosperity from a voyage by sea.

MAD. To dream you are mad, or that you are in company with mad people, is very good to the dreamer ; it promises long life, riches, happy marriage, success in trade, and good children ; if you are a farmer, some accident will happen to a part of your live stock, but will have plentiful crops : if you have a law-suit, it will be determined greatly in your favor.

MARRIAGE. To dream you are married, is ominous of death, and very unfavorable to the dreamer ; it denotes poverty, a prison, and misfortunes. To dream you assist at a wedding, is the forerunner of some pleasing news and great success. To dream of lying with your newly married husband or wife, threatens danger and sudden misfortunes, and also that you will lose a part of your property; to the sailor, it argues storms and shipwrecks, with a narrow escape from death.

MONKEYS. To dream of these mischievous creatures, is ominous of evil : they announce deceit in love ; unfaithfulness in the married state; undutiful children ; malicious enemies ; and an attack by thieves.

MOON. To dream of the moon is a very favorable omen, it denotes sudden and unexpected joy : great success in love, and that the dreamer is tenderly beloved. To dream of seeing the new moon is good for tradesmen, farmers, and lovers ; it is the forerunner of success and happiness.

MOUNTAINS. To dream you see steep and craggy mountains, presage difficulties in accomplishing your designs; if you ascend them and gain the top, you will be successful in whatever you undertake, become very rich, and arrive at great honors in the state : to a maid they denote that she will marry a man who will become rich and powerful, and that her children will be people of consequence.

MUSIC. To dream you hear delicious music, is a very favorable omen, it denotes joyful news from a long absent friend : to married people, it denotes sweet-tempered children ; in love, it shows that your sweeheart is very fond of you, is good-tempered, sincere and constant. Rough and discordant music foretells trouble, vexation, and disappointment.

NIGHTINGALE. To dream of this pretty warbler is the forerunner of joyful news : great success in business: of plentiful crops, and of a sweet tempered lover. For a married woman to dream of a nightingale, show that she will have children, who will be great singers.

ORCHARD. To dream you are in an orchard, denotes that you will become rich by the inheritance of a good legacy : that you will marry much to your advantage. For a married person to dream of being in an orchard, shows an increase of children, and that they will become rich and live happy ; it also denotes that you will have a son that will rise to a great preferment in the state, and be a great friend to the poor : in love, it denotes affection and constancy in your sweetheart, and that you will travel before you marry.

OWL. To dream of this bird of night is a very bad omen, it foretells sickness, poverty, imprisonment, and want of success in your undertakings ; it also forewarns you that some male friend will turn out perfidious, and endeavor to do you a very great injury, in which, without the utmost caution on your part he will succeed.

PEACOCK. To dream of seeing this beautiful bird is a very good omen, it denotes great success in trade : to a man, a very beautiful wife, much riches, and a good place ; to a maid, a good and rich husband : to a widow, that she will be courted by one who will tell her many fine tales, without being sincere : it also denotes great prosperity by sea, and a handsome wife in a distant part.

PIGEONS. To dream you see pigeons flying, imports hasty news of a very pleasant nature, and great success in your undertakings : they are very favorable to lovers, as they announce constancy in your sweetheart, but also that the person you love will be absent from you a long while on a journey : if your lover is at sea, they denote that he has a pleasant voyage, continues faithful, and will return rich.

PIT. To dream of falling into a deep pit, shows that some very heavy misfortune is about to attend you : that your sweetheart is false, and prefers another ; to a sailor, it forebodes some sad disaster at the next port you touch at. To dream you are in a pit, and that you climb out of it without much trouble, foreshows that you will have many enemies, and experience much trouble, but that you will overcome them and surmount your difficulties, marry well, and become rich :' to a sailor, it denotes that he will experience shipwreck, and be cast on a foreign shore, where he will be hospitably received, fall in love, and marry a rich and handsome wife, quit the sea, and live at ease on shore.

RACING. To dream you are running a race, is a token of good, presages much success in life, and that you will speedily hear some joyful news : in love it denotes that you will conquer all your rivals, and be happy in the union with the object of your affections. To dream you are riding a race, shows disappointment and anger, bad success in trade and in love : to a married woman, it denotes the loss of her husband's affection, and that her children will be in trouble.

RAIN. To dream of being in a shower of rain if it be gentle and soft, denotes great success in your present undertakings : it is particularly favorable to lovers, as it denotes constancy, affection, and a sweet temper : to the sailor, it promises good fortune by sea, and that he will marry a beautiful girl, be happy, and have children : if it be very heavy rain, accompanied with thunder and lightning, then expect to be assailed by thieves, to experience disappointments and misfortunes : such a dream denotes inconstancy and perfidy in your lover, and that another is preferred.

RAINBOW. To dream you see a rainbow, denotes great traveling and change of fortune : it also foretells sudden news of a very agreeable nature : it announces that your sweetheart is of a good temper and very constant, and that you will be very happy in marriage : great success in business through the means of trading with foreign parts.

RAVENS. To dream you see a raven, is a very unfavorable token, it denotes mischief and adversity : in love, it shows falsehood, and to the married they forebode much mischief through the adultery of your conjugal partner ; to the sailor, they betoken shipwreck, and much distress on a foreign shore.

ROSES. To dream of those fragrant flowers during the season which brings them forth, is a certain token of happiness and success : in love, they show your sweetheart to be faithful, and that you will marry and have many children : to the sailor, they indicate a pleasant and prosperous voyage with some unexpected good fortune at sea ; to the tradesman and farmer, increase of business and abundant crops. If a married woman dreams of them, she will be shortly with child of a son, who will become a great man, and render his parents very happy ; to a maiden they show her sweetheart to be industrious, and one calculated to make her very happy in the connubial state. To dream of these flowers when out of season, indicates distress and disappointment : to the tradesman they forebode bankruptcy and a prison : to the married, loss of their mates and children ; to the sailor, shipwreck and storms; to the farmer, bad crops, to the lover, infidelity in your sweetheart.

RIVER. To dream you see a flowing river, and that the waters are smooth and clear, presages happiness and success in life : to the lover, it shows constancy and affection in the object of your love, and that, if you marry, you will pass a very contented and happy life, have fine children, mostly girls, who will be very beautiful : to the tradesman and farmer, it shows prosperity and gain ; to the sailor, that his sweetheart will be kind and constant, and that his next voyage will be lucrative and pleasant. If the water appears disturbed and muddy, or has a yellow tinge, then it denotes that you will go to sea, where you will acquire considerable riches. If you have a law-suit, such a dream surely foretells that you will gain your case.

SHAVING. To dream you are being shaved, or that your head has been shaved, is a very unfavorable omen: in love, it denotes treachery and disappointment: and in the married state, infidelity and discord: to the tradesman, it argues loss of goods and business: to the sailor, an unpleasant and stormy voyage, and that he will be defrauded on a foreign shore: if you have a law-suit, it shows you that you are sold by your attorney, and will surely lose your cause: to the farmer, it prefigures bad crops and diseases amongst his live stock, also that he will be tricked by sharpers at a fair.

SHEEP. To dream you see a flock of sheep feeding, is a favorable omen, it denotes success in life; to the lover, it indicates your sweetheart to be faithful, of an amiable temper, and inclined to marry you: in the married state it denotes children, who will be very happy, become rich, and be great comforts in the evening of life: to the tradesman, it foretells increase of business and accumulation of wealth, but also forewarns him that he has a servant unworthy of his confidence: to the sailor, nothing can be a greater sign of good luck, his next voyage will be pleasant and lucrative, and his sweetheart kind and true. To dream you see them dispersing, and running away from you, shows that pretended friends are endeavoring to do you an injury, and that your children will meet with persecution and great troubles: in love, such a dream shows your sweetheart to be fickle, and little calculated to make you happy. To dream you see sheep shearing, is indicative of loss of property, and the affections of the person you love, also of your liberty. To dream you are shearing them yourself, shows that you will gain an advantage over some person who meant to harm you, and that you will get the better of difficulties, and marry the object of your affections.

SHOES. To dream you have a new pair of shoes, denotes much success in life, and triumph over your enemies; in love, they prognosticate speedy marriage and infidelity. In the married state, an increase of children. If a maiden dream she has a new pair of shoes, it denotes that a man will attempt to be rude with her, but that her honor will be saved by the interposition of a stranger, who will either marry her, or some friend of hers. To dream your shoes are worn out and bad, shows decay in circumstances and loss of friends, in love, it foretells the infidelity of your lover, who will marry another. After such a dream I advise those who can, to change their place of residence, their present situation being hereby denoted to be unfavorable for them.

SHOOTING. To dream you are out a shooting, is very favorable if you kill much game: to the lover, it shows a mistress kind and goodhumored, who will make him an excellent and notable wife: to the tradesman and farmer, success and riches: to the sailor, wealth acquired in a distant country: but if you dream you kill little or no game, then it presages bad luck, and disappointment in love. To dream you are shooting with a bow and arrows, is a very favorable dream, particularly to lovers and tradesmen.

SILK. To dream you see silk, either in pieces or for sewing, signifies prosperity, and success in undertakings; to the lover, it denotes a sweetheart of an industrious disposition, good tempered, and very faithful: in trade, it foretells increase of business, by means of women. To dream you are clothed in silk, foretells that you will rise to honors in the state, and become rich, but that you will quarrel with a rich neighbor, who will endeavor to do you mischief. For a married woman to dream of being dressed in a silk gown, shows her husband is fond of a harlot, who will go near to ruin him. If a maiden dreams of it, she will speedily see her lover.

SILVER. To dream of this valuable metal, shows that false friends are about you, and will attempt your ruin: in love, it denotes falsehood in your sweetheart. To dream you are receiving or picking up pieces of silver money, if they are small as sixpences, denotes want and a prison; if they are shillings, they indicate the receipt of a small sum of money, and the acquisition of some new friends: but if they are half-crowns, or crown-pieces, then they denote misery, a prison, and bad success in your undertakings, disappointment in your love, and loss of law-suits, attacks from thieves, and bankruptcy in trade. If a woman with child dreams of silver, it shows she will have a girl, and a good time, but the child will grow poor.

SINGING. To dream you are singing, shows that you will hear shortly some very melancholy news: to the lover, it denotes your sweetheart to be bad tempered, and of an unfaithful disposition: to the tradesman, it denotes losses by sharpers: to the farmer, loss by a hay-rick taking fire: to the sailor storms and shipwreck. To dream you only hear singing and merry making, shows that you will have some agreeable news from a person long absent: if you are in a prison, it foretells you will speedily regain your liberty.

SMALL-POX. To dream that you or your children have the small-pox, shows that you will accumulate great riches by dirty and disgraceful means, and that you will hear from a long absent friend, who is in confinement: to the lover, it denotes marriage.

SNAKES. To dream you see snakes or serpents, shows that you will be imprisoned and encounter many dangers: if you are in love, your sweetheart will be false. To dream you kill a snake, shows you will overcome difficulties and enemies, and be successful in love, trade, or farming; but unsuccessful at sea.

SNOW. To dream you see the ground covered with snow, or that it is snowing, is a very favorable dream: to a young man, it shows he will shortly marry a virgin, who is very fond of him, and that he will have children by her, chiefly girls: to a young woman, it foretells she will marry a rich man, that he will have children by her, who will become very affluent and rise to honors in the state: to the farmer, it shows plentiful crops and increase of live stock: to the tradesman, it argues great increase of buisness; to the sailor, a pleasant and very lucrative voyage, and a rich sweetheart in a foreign port. If you are soliciting a place, this dream presages that you will obtain it; if you have a lawsuit, you will gain it.

SOLDIERS. To see soldiers in your dream, shows troubles, persecution, and law suits: to the lover, they denote that the object of your affections will be obliged to quit their present place of residence by command of a father, on your account: to the tradesman, they presage loss of goods, and quarrels with creditors. To dream they are pursuing you, shows that you will be imprisoned, and meet with heavy losses, and be much disliked by your rich neighbors. This is one of those dreams after which I would advise the party dreaming to change their quarters.

SPIT. To dream you are in a kitchen turning a spit, is the forerunner of troubles and misfortunes; expect to be robbed, to lose your trade, to become very poor, and that your friends will desert you: if you are in love, it shows the object of your affections to be of a bad temper, lazy, and doomed to poverty and misfortune.

SQUIRREL. To dream of a squirrel, shows that enemies are endeavoring to slander your reputation: to the lover, it shows your sweetheart is of a bad temper, and much given to drinking: if you have a law-suit, it will surely be decided against you: if you are in trade, sharpers will endeavor to defraud you; and you will quarrel with your principal creditor.

STARCHING. To dream you are starching of linen shows you will be married to an industrious person, and that you will be successful in life, and save money; it also shows that you are about to receive a letter, containing some pleasing news.

STARS. To dream you see stars shining very bright argues success to the lover and good news from a far distant country: to the farmer, they are forerunners of a good crop: to the tradesman, great increase of business: to the sailor, a speedy marriage to a woman with money. If you dream that they are very dim and scarcely to be seen, then expect some very heavy calamity, and many severe disappointments.

STRANGE PLACE. To dream of being in a strange place denotes a good legacy from a relation whilst you are in prison: to the lover, they show inconstancy and want of affection in the object of your love, to the sailor, sickness on his next voyage.

SUN. To dream you see the sun shine, shows accumulation of riches, and enjoying posts of honor in the state, also success to the lover. To dream you see the sun rise promises fidelity in your sweetheart and good news from friends. To dream you see the sun set, shows infidelity in your sweetheart, and disgraceful news; to the tradesman, loss of business. To dream you see the sun under a cloud, foretells many hardships and troubles are about to befall you, and that you will encounter some great danger.

SWALLOWS. To dream of these harbingers of summer is a very favorable omen: they denote success in trade, and riches to the dreamer: in love they denote a speedy marriage with the object of your affections.

SWANS. To dream of seeing swans, denotes content in the marriage state, and many children; who will do well and become rich, and fill your old age with joy and happiness: to the lover, they denote constancy and affection in your sweetheart: in trade, they show success, but much vexation from the disclosure of secrets.

SWIMMING. To dream you are swimming with your head above the water, denotes great success in your undertakings, whether they be love, trade, sea or farming. To dream you are swimming with your head under water, shows that you will experience some great trouble, and hear some very unpleasant news from a person you thought dead—in trade, it shows loss of business, and that you will perhaps, be imprisoned for debt—in love, it denotes disappointment.

TEMPESTS. To dream you are in a storm or tempest, shows that you will after many difficulties, arrive at being very happy, that you will become rich, and marry well. For a lover to dream of being in a tempest, denotes that you will have many rivals, who, after causing you a great deal of vexation, you will triumph over. It also foretells, that you will receive good news from a long absent friend, who will have overcome many difficulties.

TEETH. To dream you lose a tooth, denotes the loss of some friend by death, and that troubles and misfortunes are about to attend you: to the lover, it shows the loss of your sweetheart's affection. To dream you cut a new tooth, denotes the birth of a child, who will make a great figure in the world.

THUNDER AND LIGHTNING. To dream you hear thunder or see lightning, is a very good dream; it denotes success in trade; good crops to the farmer, and a speedy and happy marriage to the lover; if you are soliciting a place, you will obtain it; if you have a law-suit, it will go in your favor; it also indicates speedy news from a far distant country.

TOADS. To dream you see these venomous reptiles, argues evil to the dreamer, they show enemies, and disappointment among friends: to the lover it denotes infidelity in your sweetheart: in trade, loss by swindlers, and spoiling of goods. To dream you kill a toad, denotes that you will overcome an enemy, and discover a person who is robbing you, and in whom you place great confidence.

TOMBS. To dream of being amongst the tombs, denotes a speedy marriage, great success in business, and the gaining of a lawsuit; also the birth of children, and unexpected news.

TREASURE. To dream you find a treasure in the earth is very ominous; it shows that you will be betrayed by some one whom you make your bosom friend; that your sweetheart is unfaithful, and grossly deceives you: if you should not be able to carry it away, then it denotes that you will have some very heavy loss: that if you have a lawsuit, it will go against you by the treachery of your attorney; and that you will be way-laid by robbers, who will ill-treat you.

TREES. To dream you see trees in blossom, denotes a happy marriage with the present object of your affections, and many children, who will do extremely well in life: to the tradesman, it denotes success in business: and to the sailor, pleasant and lucrative voyages. To dream you are climbing trees, denotes that you will make a fortune, and rise to honors and dignities in the state. To dream you are cutting down trees, fortells heavy losses by trade, and by sea; and also the death of a near relation, or dear friend.

TURNIPS. To dream of being in a turnip field, or that you see this wholesome vegetable, denotes acquisition of riches, and high employments in the state: to the lover they argue great fidelity, and an exceeding good temper in your sweetheart, and that if you marry you will be very happy, have fine children, and thrive in the world.

TRUMPET. To dream you hear the sound of a trumpet, is a bad omen, and denotes troubles and misfortunes; to the tradesman, it presages the loss of business; to the farmer, bad crops; to the lover, insincerity in the object of his affections.

WALLS. To dream you are walking on crazy old and narrow walls, denotes that you will engage in some very dangerous enterprise, that will cause you much trouble and vexation: if you get down without hurting yourself, or the wall's falling, then you will succeed: if the wall should fall whilst you are upon it, you will be disappointed: if you are walking between walls, and the passage is very narrow and difficult, you will be engaged in some quarrel, or other disagreeable affair, from which it will require great circumspection and caution on your part to disengage yourself, but if you get from between them safe, you will, after some difficulties, settle well in life, marry an agreeable partner, have children, and become rich and happy.

WALKING. To dream you are walking in a dirty, muddy place, foretells sickness and vexation: to the lover, it denotes your sweetheart to be bad tempered and unfaithful; to the tradesman, it fortells dishonest servants, and loss of goods by fire.

WATER. To dream you are drinking water, denotes great trouble and adversity: in trade, loss of business, and being arrested: to the lover, it shows your sweetheart is false, prefers another, and will never marry you.

WATER-MILL. To dream of being in a water-mill is a favorable omen: to the tradesman, it denotes great increase of business: to the farmer, abundant crops: in love, success, a rich sweetheart, and a happy marriage.

WEDDING. To dream of being married, or at a wedding, is a very unfavorable dream, especially for lovers; it denotes the death of some dear friend or relation, with loss of property, and severe disappointment.

WHEAT. To dream you see, or are walking in a field of wheat, is a very favorable omen, and denotes great prosperity and riches: in love, it argues a completion of your most sanguine wishes, and fortells much happiness, with fine children when you marry: if you have a lawsuit, you will gain it, and you will be successful in all your undertakings.

WOOD. To dream you are cutting or chopping of wood, shows that you will be happy in your family, and become rich and respectable in life. To dream you are carrying wood on your back shows that you will rise to affluence by your industry, but that your partner will be of a bad temper, and your children undutiful. If you dream you are walking in an extensive wood, it denotes that you will quickly fall in love, and also that you will be often married.

WOOL. To dream you are buying or selling of wool, denotes prosperity and great affluence, by means of industry and trade: to the lover, it is a favorable omen; your sweetheart is thereby shown to be of an amiable disposition, very constant, and deeply in love with you. To dream of having wool on your head instead of hair, betokens a severe fit of illness, and unpleasant news from a far distant country.

WOUNDS. To dream you are wounded, is a very favorable omen, especially if it be with a sword; to the lover, it denotes success in your amours, and with an agreeable partner, who will be faithful and affectionate : to the tradesman, profit and increase of business : to the farmer, an increase in his cattle and plentiful crops : to the sailor a profitable voyage, with unexpected success in love.

YARROW. To dream of this weed, which is in general most abundant in church yards, denotes to the married, deaths in the family ; and to the single, that the grim tyrant will deprive them of the first object on whom they rest their affections.

YEW-TREE. An indication of the funeral of a very aged person, by whose death the dreamer will derive some benefit, or a protecting hand among the relations of the deceased person.

YEWBERRIES. To a young man it shows a great disappointment in setting out in life ; and to a young maiden it predicts dishonor if she gathers them, particularly if they stain any part of her clothes or hands.

ZEALANDER. To dream you see an Indian, in his native dress, shows to a man he will travel, and to a woman she will wed a foreigner. To dream you see an Indian female, predicts to a man that he will wed a rich widow, and to a woman, that she will have a son who will raise himself to great power and honor in the Indies, and bring wealth and honor to his kindred.

THE ORACULUM;

OR,

BOOK OF· FATE:

CONSULTED BY

NAPOLEON BONAPARTE.

The Oraculum is gifted with every requisite variety of response to the following questions :

1. Shall I obtain my wish ?
2. Shall I have success in my undertakings ?
3. Shall I gain or lose in my cause ?
4. Shall I have to live in foreign parts ?
5. Will the stranger return ?
6. Shall I recover my property ?
7. Will my friend be true ?
8. Shall I have to travel ?
9. Does the person love and regard me ?
10. Will the marriage be prosperous ?
11. What sort of a wife, or husband, shall I have ?
12. Will she have a son or daughter ?
13. Will the patient recover ?
14. Will the prisoner be released ?
15. Shall I be lucky or unlucky ?
16. What does my dream signify ?

HOW TO WORK THE ORACULUM.

MAKE marks in four lines, one under another, in the following manner, making more or less in each line, according to your fancy :—

```
* * * * * * * *
* * * * * * * * *
* * * * * * * * * *
* * * * * * * * * * *
```

Then reckon the number of marks in each line, and ·if it be *odd*, mark down one dot ; if *even*, two dots. If there be more than nine marks, reckon the surplus ones over that number only : viz.,

The number of marks in the first line of the foregoing are *odd* ; therefore make one mark, thus . . . .   *

In the second, *even*, so make two, thus * *
In the third, *odd* again, make one mark only . . . .   *
In the fourth, *even* again, two marks   * *

TO OBTAIN THE ANSWER.

You must refer to THE ORACULUM, at the top of which you will find a row of dots similar to those you have produced, and a column of figures corresponding with those prefixed to the questions : guide your eye down the column at the top of which you find the dots resembling your own, till you come to the letter on a line with the number of the question you are trying ; then refer to the page having that letter at the top, and on a line with the dots which are similar to your own, you will find your *answer.*

The following are unlucky days, on which none of the questions should be worked, or any enterprise undertaken : Jan. 1, 2, 4, 6, 10, 20, 22 ; Feb. 6, 17, 28 ; Mar. 24, 26 ; April 10, 27, 28 ; May 7, 8 ; June 27 ; July 17, 21 ; Aug. 20, 22 ; Sept. 5, 30 ; Oct. 6 ; Nov. 3, 29 ; Dec. 6, 10, 15.

˚* It is not right to try a question twice in one day.

ORACULUM.

Num.	QUESTIONS.																	Num.
1	Shall I obtain my wish?	A	B	C	D	E	F	G	H	I	K	L	M	N	O	P	Q	1
2	Shall I have success in my undertakings?	B	C	D	E	F	G	H	I	K	L	M	N	O	P	Q	A	2
3	Shall I gain or lose in my cause?	C	D	E	F	G	H	I	K	L	M	N	O	P	Q	A	B	3
4	Shall I have to live in foreign parts?	D	E	F	G	H	I	K	L	M	N	O	P	Q	A	B	C	4
5	Will the stranger return from abroad?	E	F	G	H	I	K	L	M	N	O	P	Q	A	B	C	D	5
6	Shall I recover my property stolen?	F	G	H	I	K	L	M	N	O	P	Q	A	B	C	D	E	6
7	Will my friend be true in his dealings?	G	H	I	K	L	M	N	O	P	Q	A	B	C	D	E	F	7
8	Shall I have to travel?	H	I	K	L	M	N	O	P	Q	A	B	C	D	E	F	G	8
9	Does the person love and regard me?	I	K	L	M	N	O	P	Q	A	B	C	D	E	F	G	H	9
10	Will the marriage be prosperous?	K	L	M	N	O	P	Q	A	B	C	D	E	F	G	H	I	10
11	What sort of wife or husband shall I have?	L	M	N	O	P	Q	A	B	C	D	E	F	G	H	I	K	11
12	Will she have a son, or a daughter?	M	N	O	P	Q	A	B	C	D	E	F	G	H	I	K	L	12
13	Will the patient recover from his illness?	N	O	P	Q	A	B	C	D	E	F	G	H	I	K	L	M	13
14	Will the prisoner be released?	O	P	Q	A	B	C	D	E	F	G	H	I	K	L	M	N	14
15	Shall I be lucky, or unlucky this day?	P	Q	A	B	C	D	E	F	G	H	I	K	L	M	N	O	15
16	What does my dream signify?	Q	A	B	C	D	E	F	G	H	I	K	L	M	N	O	P	16

	A.		B.
* * * *	What you wish for, you will shortly OBTAIN.	* * * *	The luck that is ordained for you will be coveted by others.
** * ** *	Signifies trouble and sorrow.	** * **	Whatever your desires are, for the present decline them.
* * * *	Be very cautious what you do THIS day, lest trouble befall you.	* ** * *	Signifies a favor of kindness from some person.
** * * **	The prisoner DIES, and is regretted by his friends.	** * * **	There ARE enemies, who would defraud and render you unhappy.
** ** ** *	Life will be spared THIS time, to prepare for death.	** ** ** *	With great difficulty he will obtain pardon or release again.
** * **	A very handsome daughter, but a PAINFUL one.	** * **	The patient should be prepared to LEAVE this world.
** * * *	You will have a virtuous woman or man, for your wife or husband.	** * *	She will have a SON, who will be learned and wise.
** * * *	If you marry THIS person, you will have enemies where you little expect.	** ** *	A RICH partner is ordained for you.
* * ** **	You had better decline THIS love, for it is neither constant nor true.	* ** **	By THIS marriage you will have great luck and prosperity.
* * * **	DECLINE your travels, for they will not be to your advantage.	* * **	THIS love comes from an upright and sincere heart.
** * ** **	There is a true and sincere friendship between you BOTH.	** * **	God WILL surely travel with you, and bless you.
* ** ** **	You will NOT recover the stolen property.	* ** **	Beware of friends who are false and deceitful.
* ** ** *	The stranger WILL, with joy, soon return.	* ** *	You WILL recover your property—unexpectedly.
* ** *	You will NOT remove from where you are at present.	* ** *	Love prevents his return home at present.
* ** * **	The Lord WILL support you in a good cause.	* ** * **	Your stay is NOT here: be therefore prepared for a change.
** ** ** **	You are NOT lucky—pray to God that he may help you.	** ** ** **	You will have NO GAIN; therefore be wise and careful.

C.	**D.**
With the blessing of God you WILL have great gain.	You WILL obtain a great fortune in another country.
Very unlucky indeed—pray to God for his assistance.	By venturing freely, you WILL certainly gain doubly.
If your desires are NOT extravagant, they will be granted.	God WILL change your misfortune into success and happiness.
Signifies peace and plenty between friends.	Alter your intentions or else you MAY meet poverty and distress.
Be well prepared THIS day, or you may meet with trouble.	Signifies you have many impediments in accomplishing your pursuits.
The prisoner WILL find it difficult to obtain his pardon or release.	Whatever may possess your inclinations this day, abandon them.
The patient WILL YET enjoy health and prosperity.	The prisoner WILL get free again this time.
She WILL have a daughter, and will require attention.	The patient's illness WILL be lingering and doubtful.
The person has NOT a great fortune but is in middling circumstances.	She will have a dutiful and handsome son.
Decline THIS marriage, or else you may be sorry.	The person will be LOW in circumstances, but honest-hearted.
Decline a courtship which MAY be your destruction.	A marriage which WILL ADD to your welfare and prosperity.
Your travels are IN VAIN: you had better stay at home.	You love a person who does not speak well of you.
You MAY DEPEND on a true and sincere friendship.	Your travels WILL be prosperous, if guided by prudence.
You must NOT expect to regain that which you have lost.	He means NOT what he says, for his heart is false.
SICKNESS prevents the traveler from seeing you.	With some trouble and expense, you may regain your property.
It WILL be your fate to stay where you now are.	You must NOT expect to see the stranger again.

E.

* The stranger WILL NOT return so soon as you expect.

* Remain among your friends, and you will do well.

* You will hereafter GAIN what you seek.

* You have NO LUCK—pray to God, and strive honestly.

* You will obtain your wishes by means of a friend.

* Signifies you have enemies who will endeavor to ruin you.

* Beware—an enemy is endeavoring to bring you to strife and misfortune.

* The prisoner's sorrow and anxiety are great, and his release uncertain.

* The patient WILL soon recover—there is no danger.

* She will have a daughter, who will be honored and respected.

* Your partner WILL be fond of liquor, and will debase himself thereby.

* This marriage will bring you to poverty, be therefore discreet.

* Their love is false to you, and true to others.

* DECLINE you travels for the present, for they will be dangerous.

* THIS person is serious and true, and deserves to be respected.

* You will not recover the property you have lost.

F.

* By persevering you WILL recover your property again.

* It is out of the stranger's power to return.

* You will GAIN, and be successful in foreign parts.

* A great fortune is ordained for you; wait patiently.

* There is great hindrance to your success at present.

* Your wishes are in VAIN at present.

* Signifies there is sorrow and danger before you.

* THIS day is unlucky; therefore, alter you intention.

* The prisoner will be restored to liberty and freedom.

* The patient's recovery is doubtful.

* She will have a very fine BOY.

* A worthy person, and a fine fortune.

* Your intentions would destroy your rest and peace.

* THIS love is true and constant; forsake it not.

* PROCEED on your journey, and you will not have cause to repent it.

* If you trust THIS friend, you may have cause for sorrow.

G.	H.
This friend exceeds all others in every respect.	Commence your travels, and they will go on as you could wish.
You must bear your loss with fortitude.	Your pretended friend hates you secretely.
The stranger will return unexpectedly.	Your hopes to recover your property are vain.
Remain at HOME with your friends, and you will escape misfortunes.	A certain affair prevents the stranger's return immediately.
You will meet no GAIN in your pursuits.	Your fortune you will find in abundance abroad.
Heaven will bestow its blessings on you.	Decline the pursuit, and you will do well.
No.	Your expectations are vain—you will not succeed.
Signifies that you will shortly be out of the POWER of your enemies.	You will obtain what you wish for.
ILL-LUCK awaits you—it will be difficult for you to escape it.	Signifies that on this day your fortune will change for the better.
The prisoner will be RELEASED by death only.	Cheer up your spirits, your luck is at hand.
By the blessing of God, the patient WILL recover.	After LONG imprisonment he will be released.
A daughter, but of a very sickly contution.	The patient will he relieved from sickness.
You will get an honest, young, and handsome partner.	She will have a healthy SON.
Decline this marriage, else it may be to your sorrow.	You will be married to your equal in a short time.
Avoid this love.	If you wish to be happy, do not marry this person.
Prepare for a short journey; you will be recalled by unexpected events.	This love is from the heart, and will continue until death.

I.

The love is great, but it will cause great jealousy.

It will be in vain for you to travel.

Your friend will be as sincere as you could wish him to be.

You will recover the stolen property through a cunning person.

The traveler will soon return with joy.

You will not be prosperous or fortunate in foreign parts.

Place your trust in GOD, who is the disposer of happiness.

Your fortune will shortly be changed into misfortune.

You will succeed as you desire.

Signifies that the misfortune which threatens will be prevented.

Beware of your enemies, who seek to do you harm.

After a short time your anxiety for the prisoner will cease.

God will give the patient health and strength again.

She will have a very fine daughter.

You will marry a person with whom you will have little comfort.

The marriage will not answer your expectations.

K.

After much misfortune you will be comfortable and happy.

A sincere love from an upright heart.

You will be prosperous in your journey.

Do not RELY on the friendship of this person.

The property is lost for EVER; but the thief will be punished.

The traveler will be absent some considerable time.

You will meet luck and happiness in a foreign country.

You will not have any success for the present.

You will succeed in your undertaking.

Change your intentions, and you will do well.

Signifies that there are rogues at hand.

Be reconciled, your circumstances will shortly mend.

The prisoner will be released.

The patient will depart this life.

She will have a son.

It will be difficult for you to get a partner.

	L.		M.
✳✳✳	You will get a very handsome person for your partner.	✳✳✳	She will have a son, who will gain wealth and honor.
✳✳ ✳ ✳✳ ✳	Various misfortunes will attend this marriage.	✳✳✳ ✳ ✳✳✳	You will get a partner with great undertakings and much money.
✳✳ ✳	This love is whimsical and changeable.	✳✳✳ ✳	The marriage will be prosperous.
✳✳✳ ✳ ✳✳	You will be unlucky in your travels.	✳✳ ✳ ✳✳	She, or He, wishes to be yours this moment.
✳✳ ✳✳ ✳	This person's love is just and true. You may rely on it.	✳✳ ✳✳ ✳✳	Your journey will prove to your advantage.
✳✳ ✳ ✳✳	You will lose, but the thief will suffer most.	✳✳ ✳ ✳✳	Place no great trust in that person.
✳✳ ✳ ✳	The stranger will soon return with plenty.	✳✳✳ ✳ ✳	You will find your property at a certain time.
✳✳ ✳ ✳	If you remain at home, you will have success.	✳✳ ✳ ✳	The traveler's return is rendered doubtful by his conduct.
✳ ✳✳ ✳✳	Your gain will be trivial.	✳ ✳✳	You will succeed as you desire in foreign parts.
✳ ✳ ✳ ✳✳	You will meet sorrow and trouble.	✳ ✳ ✳✳	Expect no gain; it will be in vain.
✳✳ ✳ ✳✳ ✳✳	You will succeed according to your wishes.	✳✳✳ ✳ ✳✳	You will have more LUCK than you expect.
✳ ✳✳ ✳✳	Signifies that you will get money.	✳ ✳✳ ✳✳	Whatever your desires are, you will speedily obtain them.
✳ ✳✳ ✳	In spite of enemies, you will do well.	✳ ✳✳ ✳✳	Signifies you will be asked to a wedding.
✳ ✳✳ ✳	The prisoner will pass many days in confinement.	✳ ✳✳ ✳	You will have no occasion to complain of ill-luck.
✳✳ ✳ ✳✳	The patient will recover.	✳✳ ✳ ✳	Some one will pity and release the prisoner.
✳✳ ✳✳ ✳✳	She will have a daughter.	✳✳ ✳✳ ✳✳	The patient's recovery is unlikely.

N.	O.
The patient will recover, but his days are short.	The prisoner will be released with joy.
She will have a daughter.	The patient's recovery is doubtful.
You will marry into a very respectable family.	She will have a son, who will live to a great age.
By this marriage you will gain nothing.	You will get a virtuous partner.
Await the time and you will find the love great.	Delay not this marriage—you will meet much happiness.
Venture not from home.	None loves you better in this world.
This person is a sincere friend.	You may proceed with confidence.
You will never recover the theft.	Not a friend, but a secret enemy.
The stranger will return, but not quickly.	You will soon recover what is stolen.
When abroad, keep from evil women or they will do you harm.	The stranger will not return again.
You will soon gain what you little expect.	A foreign woman will greatly enhance your fortune.
You will have great success.	You will be cheated out of your gain.
Rejoice ever at that which is ordained for you.	Your misfortunes will vanish and you will be happy.
Signifies that sorrow will depart, and joy will return.	Your hope is in vain—fortune shuns you at present.
Your luck is in blossom; it will soon be at hand.	That you will soon hear agreeable news.
Death may end the imprisonment.	There are misfortunes lurking about you.

	P.
* * * *	This day brings you an increase of happiness.
** * **	The prisoner will quit the power of his enemies.
** * * *	The patient will recover and live long.
** * **	She will have two daughters.
** ** ** *	A rich young person will be your partner.
** * **	Hasten your marriage—it will bring you much happiness.
** * * *	The person loves you sincerely.
** * * *	You will not prosper from home.
* ** **	This friend is more valuable than gold.
* * **	You will NEVER receive your goods.
** * ** **	He is dangerously ill, and cannot yet return.
* ** **	Depend upon your own industry, and remain at home.
* ** *	Be joyful, for future prosperity is ordained for you.
* ** *	Depend not too much on your good luck.
* ** * **	What you wish will be granted to you.
** ** ** **	That you should be very careful this day, lest any accident befall you.

	Q.
* * *	Signifies much joy and happiness between friends.
** * ** *	This day is not very lucky, but rather the reverse.
** * *	He will yet come to honor, although he now suffers.
** * **	Recovery is doubtful; therefore, be prepared for the worst.
** ** *	She will have a son who will prove forward.
** * **	A rich partner, but a bad temper.
* * *	By wedding this person you insure your happiness.
** * *	The person has great love for you, but wishes to conceal it.
* ** **	You may proceed on your journey without fear.
* * **	Trust him not; he is inconstant and deceitful.
* * **	In a very singular manner you will recover your property.
* ** **	The stranger will return very soon.
* ** *	You will dwell abroad in comfort and happiness.
* ** *	If you will deal fairly you will surely prosper.
* ** *	You will yet live in spendor and plenty.
** ** **	Make yourself contented with your PRESENT fortune.